HOUSE PARTY MURDER RAP

A 1920S HISTORICAL COZY MYSTERY - AN EVIE PARKER MYSTERY BOOK 1

SONIA PARIN

vJan2020

ISBN: 9781792903540

CHAPTER 1

The talk of the town

Spring, 1920
Hainsley Hall, Yarborough, Yorkshire

$\mathcal{L}$ ady Wainscot settled down to read the missive which had been delivered earlier that day. Her morning had been filled with last minute preparations for that weekend's house party and she'd only now managed to find the time to attend to other matters.

Her eyes widened with each word she read.

"So, it's true," she murmured to herself. "Evangeline Parker will be arriving this afternoon." Her lips pursed with obvious dissatisfaction. She had heard a rumor, but she hadn't thought it possible.

Actually, she hadn't wanted to believe it.

Not only had Evangeline Parker returned from her extended trip to America, but she had also decided to revisit the scene of her crime.

This weekend, of all weekends.

Pressing her hand to her chest, Lady Wainscot drew in a sharp breath. With numerous guests arriving within the hour, she wouldn't be able to make the rounds and find out more.

Succumbing to the feeling of utter defeat, her hand dropped to her lap. A second later, she perked up. She would send someone else to make inquiries and report back to her.

Determined to take prompt action, she rang the bell. She'd expected the butler to make an appearance but, instead, the maid rushed in. She supposed it had something to do with the household being in an upheaval as everyone rushed around ensuring everything met her exacting standards.

Surging to her feet, Lady Wainscot fussed with her skirt and, lifting her chin, she straightened into her trademark imperious pose. "Ruth, would you please tell the girls to come down this instant. I need to speak with them."

"As you wish, milady."

"Tell them to hurry," Lady Wainscot urged.

"Yes, milady."

As the maid turned to leave, another thought occurred. "Ruth. Tell them they'll be riding to Yarborough Manor."

The maid's brow furrowed slightly.

"Well? Go on."

"Begging your pardon, milady. I just finished helping Miss Eugene into her new dress. It took forever to do all those little buttons up. She's not going to be pleased about having to change again... what with the guests arriving so soon..."

Lady Wainscot gave the maid a slight lift of her eyebrow, a sure sign of her displeasure and growing impatience.

"Yes, milady. Right away."

As soon as the maid disappeared to deliver her instructions, Lady Wainscot drew in a calming breath and released it as a shuddering sigh.

Evangeline Parker.

Here to ruin everything for her.

Again.

"Over my dead body."

The outskirts of Yarborough, Yorkshire

. . .

Evangeline's eyes fluttered open. It took her a moment to engage her mind. When she did, she emitted a light groan.

They were trekking through the Yorkshire countryside, making their way to Yarborough Manor for the weekend house party, one of many events in the county organized as a season opener.

If given the choice, she would much rather have stayed at the London house enjoying her semi reclusive lifestyle. However, after two months of limiting her social outings to a few dinners and afternoon teas, she had run out of excuses and so she had sat down to go through the invitations which had begun pouring in the moment she had returned to London.

She wished news about her return to England hadn't spread quite so quickly. In her opinion, this only gave rise to speculation about her reasons for returning; assumptions she could do without since they would all, no doubt, focus on her marital status...

"If only people would simply let it go," she mouthed.

Ten years before, in the spring of 1910, she had first set foot on English soil as a spirited debutante urged by her mama to make the best of her season and land herself a titled gentleman.

As a young girl, Evie had traveled the length and breadth of her homeland, including little known tracks of wilderness, and had been eager to experience something vibrantly new.

Unfortunately, she had been disappointed. Instead of the excitement she had yearned for, she had found everyone and everything in England deeply steeped in old traditions and rules. More than she had ever encountered, Evie thought. Feeling stifled, she had pleaded with her mama to take her back home, all to no avail.

Then, to her surprise, she had fallen in love and she had remained in love until destiny had dealt her a hard, cruel hand.

Everything had been altered. She had become a widow. Her first instinct had been to flee back home to America and stay there but, after two years of being cocooned in familiar surroundings, she had made the firm decision to return to England.

She had as yet to determine if this had been the right step to take. While she'd had plenty of time to get used to her new status as a single woman and to overcome the pain of her loss, which everyone had promised would subside in due course, she knew the memories would surely surge to the surface again.

Such is life, she thought and switched her attention to the here and now.

She supposed it would be fabulous to catch up with Bicky.

Albert Brenton, Duke of Hetherington, Bicky to his

close friends and family, had been her husband's oldest friend. He, of all people, would understand why she'd chosen to stay away.

"Tom?"

"Yes, ma'am."

"I slept like a log. The last time I came out to York-shire, the driver hit every pothole along the way. You are marvelous."

"Thank you, ma'am."

Evie pressed her lips together to stop herself from correcting him. Tom Winchester had been in her employ for two months and he still insisted on calling her ma'am, but at least he had stopped using her title.

She hoped she hadn't confused the situation by not providing him with an alternative form of address. For now, it would have to be ma'am. At least until she settled on something less formal. How would she feel if her chauffeur called her Evie?

Of course, despite protocol, she hadn't thought twice about embracing a first name practice. In reality, she should have addressed her chauffeur as Winchester, but Evie preferred Tom. And, in this instance, she wished to have her way—something that seemed to be happening with increasing regularity, she couldn't help thinking.

During her recent journey back home to America she had allowed all the formalities that accompanied her life in England to lapse. Perhaps a part of her had hoped Tom would help her maintain it by adopting a more casual approach. It would certainly be a lovely bridge between the life she led and the life she yearned for. Surely that had been her grandmother's intention when she'd arranged for Tom to become her chauffeur and travel back to England with her.

"Tom. Have you ever lived in the country?"

"On occasion, ma'am."

Evie waited for him to provide more information but it seemed, where his private life was concerned, he would remain a closed book.

Not if she had her way...

"Tom, I believe we are now traveling through the Duke's land. Have you ever seen anything so vast?"

Tom appeared to weigh his words before responding, "Yes, ma'am. In Texas. Although, this is much greener."

Surprised to hear more than a yes or no answer, Evie smiled.

The distraction she had sought did not last.

A sense of trepidation swept through her. The last time she had traveled this way, she had been blissfully happy...

Closing her eyes, she recalled her granny's warning to brace herself because, in her opinion, Evie's return would be seen as throwing down the gauntlet, so she shouldn't be surprised when the reprisals began shooting her way.

Young, wealthy, titled... and available.

Yes, some people would perceive her presence as flaunting her availability. However, they would be wrong.

She had no intention of marrying again.

Ever.

CHAPTER 2

The Red Sox v The Yankees

"How are you enjoying the scenery, Tom? I believe this is your first trip to the English countryside."

Several seconds ticked by before Tom answered. "It's a pleasant change from London, ma'am."

Yes, she would have to agree. A few days away from the busy and frenetic activities of town living would do her a world of good. At least, she hoped so. "Tom…"

"Yes, ma'am."

"Do you miss home?"

"I can't say that I do, ma'am."

"Really?" Whenever she came across someone from

her neck of the woods, all they could talk about was how much they missed just about everything, which made her wonder why they ever bothered making the long transatlantic journey.

"Do you follow any games, Tom?" Evie asked, although she already knew the answer. However, if she didn't encourage a conversation, he would quite happily drive the rest of the way in complete silence.

"Baseball, ma'am."

"Let me guess, you're a Yankee's fan." Leaning slightly forward, Evie saw his jaw muscles clench.

"Red Sox, ma'am."

"Oh, I beg your pardon," she said lightly. "My mistake. Of course, I'd forgotten. You originally hail from Boston." She tried to hide her smile. Her tone filled with innocence as she said, "I'm partial to the Yankees. I wonder… is this going to affect our working relationship?"

His jaw muscles twitched again. "I don't see why it should, ma'am."

Of course, it wouldn't. But she couldn't help predicting many lively conversations.

It had only been a few months since the Red Sox had shipped Babe Ruth to the Yankees in exchange for crisp stacks of redeemable U.S. currency. Many fans had been aghast that such a talent would be cast off while others had welcomed the change in favor of a more cohesive team rather than a one-man show.

Their loss and the Yankee's win, Evie thought.

"You'll have to keep me informed, Tom. Sometimes, I become so immersed in the society pages, I don't find the time to get to the sports coverage." Evie wondered if this would help lower the barrier he seemed so intent on maintaining. She hoped it would.

Leaning forward slightly, she said, "We're coming up to the village now. I want to point out the pub."

When her granny had asked her to look after Tom, Evie had taken the request to heart. So, she had sent a message ahead to organize a room for Tom at the local pub.

Servants working in large estates were used to guests bringing their own staff, but Evie had heard too many stories about servants imposing their stalwart rules of etiquette and strict class system.

Knowing Tom had never worked in service before and having her own two pennies worth of opinions about the often tedious snobbery of drawing rooms, she had decided to spare him the hierarchical down-stairs experience.

Pointing ahead, she said, "There it is. The Bow and Arrow." She caught sight of his small smile. "It's a quaint name and rather a pleasant change from the usual Royal Arms or Queen's something or other. Then again, being new to England, you might not have noticed the practice of giving pubs rather engaging names."

"Actually, I have noticed, ma'am. In fact, I was thinking of the *Hang Drawn and Quartered* or the *I Am the Only Running Footman* pubs, both in London."

"Oh, yes. That one is in Charles Street, Mayfair. And, you're right, there are some unusual names." She tapped her chin and tried to recall a few names she'd encountered during her various jaunts around the countryside. "*The Case is Altered*, in Middlesex and *The Bucket of Blood* in Cornwall come to mind." She settled back into her seat. "I believe you will find The Bow and Arrow quite comfortable."

"I'm sure I will, ma'am." He cleared his throat. "I hope I'm not speaking out of turn, but are you sure you want to dispense with my services during your stay, ma'am?"

"Yes, quite sure. These type of house parties are well orchestrated. There will be lunches and dinners and in-between, walks and rides and perhaps some shooting. All taking place within the estate. So, you see, you can enjoy a nice vacation."

As they entered the village, Tom slowed down to an appropriate speed. In previous years, Evie had been a regular guest at Yarborough Manor, the Duke of Hetherington's family seat. In fact, she had met her husband at one of Bicky's house parties.

After her marriage, there had been a number of times when they had enjoyed extended visits and Evie had often wandered around the small village, acquainting herself with some of the locals.

"Tom, could you please stop the car. I'd like to drop in on *Marceline's Salon de Beaute*. They stock the most wonderful primrose scented soap. At least, I hope they still do. I'd like to place an order."

Evie recalled *Marceline's Salon de Beaute's* humble beginnings selling anything and everything from dresses to locally made soaps as well as the emerging ladies' beauty care products. Now, it seemed, they had revamped the business, seemingly aspiring to cater to a more exclusive clientele, but in reality, netting their business from any female intent on staving off the ravages of time.

Evie strode across the square, stopping a couple of times to give way to vehicles. The last time she had visited the village, motor vehicles had been a rare sight. She spotted a horse and cart outside a store and made a point of committing the image to memory, since she doubted she would see many more in the near future.

Along the way, she exchanged smiles with the local villagers she encountered, even though she failed to recognize most of them. It didn't surprise her to see new faces as the last couple of years had introduced many changes with people moving to different towns or large cities. She had heard say some people had abandoned their lives of service and had moved on to more lucrative jobs in stores or factories.

A man tipped his hat at her. Another one stopped to let her through. She saw a man standing by Marceline's salon, the sleeve of his coat pinned up. A war casualty, Evie thought. A moment later, a lady emerged from the store and, joining him, they strode away together.

When she entered the store, a delicate doorbell announced her entrance.

"Lady Woodridge!" the young woman behind the counter exclaimed.

Evie gave her a warm smile. "Hello, Anna. You look splendid. I love your new hairstyle." The last time she'd seen her, Anna had just started out in the store and had worn her hair in braids twisted and gathered into a neat bun. Now, she sported the current Parisian rage; a fashionable bob with neat rows of delicate waves.

"Anna, I would like to order some of your lovely primrose soap. Do you still carry it?"

"Yes, indeed, milady. Would you like it sent up to the house?"

"Yes, please. I'm spending a few days at Yarborough Manor," Evie confirmed.

Anna nodded. "I'll send the delivery boy out this afternoon."

Thanking her, Evie turned to leave when she noticed an eye-catching display. "Oh, what are these?"

Anna picked up one of the tubes and presented it with a flourish. "Cupids Bow. A new shade by Helena

Rubinstein. Offering perfectly curved lips with professional deftness."

"What a marvelous shade. Include one of those too, please."

"Certainly, milady."

Evie couldn't help noticing Anna's subtle gesture toward a sign on the counter and wondered if she had employed the same subtle tactic to draw her attention to the lipstick.

"Day beauty care?" Evie asked, her voice filled with awe. "Is that a new service?"

"Yes, indeed."

"By appointment only," Evie read. "I wouldn't mind trying it." Before her journey to England, she had stopped for several days in New York and had indulged in a day of beauty at Helena Rubinstein's main salon. It had done wonders for her complexion, or so she'd been told. Her face had certainly felt pampered after the treatment. "I'll send word later on with a suitable time. Or perhaps I could decide now. Would tomorrow be too soon?"

Anna drew out an appointment book and, taking the greatest care, wrote Evie's name.

As she watched her, Evie sensed she had drawn the attention from another customer in the store. Turning slightly, Evie studied the woman. It took her a moment to place the lady who stood near a display of face creams casting furtive glances her way.

Lotte Browning, married to the local solicitor. Her father had been a Baron and she had aspired to marry a titled gentleman but, after several failed seasons, she had given up and had accepted Mr. Browning's humble proposal. According to the rumor mills, Mrs. Lotte Browning would continue to hold on to her aspirations until the day she died.

To Evie's surprise, Lotte bobbed a curtsey.

To her even greater surprise, Lotte then scurried out of the store.

Smiling, Evie returned her attention to the young salesgirl.

"It seems I have been away too long, but it's lovely to be back." Content with her purchases, Evie strode out of the store. As she crossed the square again, she noticed Lotte Browning standing nearby looking at a store window. Or rather, pretending to look while her attention clearly remained pinned on Evie.

Nothing but curiosity, Evie thought, determined she would not let it bother her, even though she had heard rumors about Lotte Browning's stalwart objections to Evie's marriage. Many had shared her sentiments. In fact, to Evie's astonishment, the news had caused ripples of discontent right across the county's drawing rooms and beyond...

About to reach the car, Evie noticed a man staring at her. When she met his gaze, he pushed off and strode off, his pace hurried. It seemed she'd attracted the attention from more than one person, she thought.

Lotte Browning remained standing by the store window which made Evie wonder what she could find so enthralling.

She smiled at Tom. "I'll only be another moment." A few steps brought her up to the store holding Lotte Browning's attention.

Farm equipment?

Evie continued on and entered the store next door, moments later, she emerged with a small bag of mints.

Lotte Browning saw her coming out and swiftly looked away.

Humming a tune under her breath, Evie returned to the car and offered Tom a mint. He shook his head and thanked her.

"Go on. Have one."

Relenting, Tom took one and held the door open for her.

Evie settled into the car and they were promptly on their way again driving through the quaint village until they were once again in the open road admiring the lush green hills of the Yorkshire countryside.

As she gazed out at the meadows, Evie thought about Lotte. She would no doubt be making haste and rushing to inform as many people as she could about the notorious Evangeline Parker's arrival in the county. Evie knew very few people, if any, would bother to use her rightful title when gossiping about her. Although, they would display all manner of politeness while out in public.

As she gazed out the passenger window, Evie thought she caught sight of a glint of light reflected from within the copse of trees lining the road.

"Tom, I think birdwatchers are out and about. I have an uncle who is as migratory as the birds he chases around the country. He simply adores his hobby."

The car moved along the winding road and onto a clearing where she saw the flash of light reflected again.

Evie guessed she had become the birdwatcher's new interest and imagined the person rushing home to declare he had personally witnessed the arrival of 'that Parker woman'.

She was about to look away when she saw a flock of birds taking flight, squawking as they flew off in an obvious state of panic. A concerned look crossed Evie's face. She leaned forward only to be jerked back when the car suddenly jolted.

In the next instant, the car swerved.

"Get down!" Tom shouted at the same time as his hand shot out, his palm extended as if to block something.

He grabbed hold of the steering wheel and brought

the car to a halt, by some miracle managing to avoid rolling into a ditch by a mere few inches.

Tom swung around to look at her. "Are you all right, ma'am?"

"Y-yes." Evie straightened and adjusted her hat. "What happened?"

Instead of answering her, Tom jumped out of the car. He rushed from one end of the vehicle to the other. Evie imagined he wanted to inspect the tires for possible damage. When he finished, he jumped in and got them moving again. Although, not at the sedate pace they'd been traveling at. Instead, the car moved at full speed.

Evie held on for dear life. She barely had time to notice Yarborough Manor coming into view before they sped past the gatehouse and along the long driveway.

"Tom?" Evie exclaimed.

Leaning forward, he looked about. Yarborough Manor sat in the middle of an expansive park but Tom's attention appeared to be speared toward the copse of trees in the distance.

He finally brought the car to a stop in front of the impressive porticoed entrance and after a few moments, his hands released their hold on the steering wheel and he sat back saying, "I'm sorry about that, ma'am. The sun hit my eyes and I lost control of the vehicle."

The sun?

When he turned, he looked at her with steady eyes as he again apologized and promised it would never happen again.

The sun...

Hit his eyes?

Evie stared right back at him and wondered why he had just lied to her.

CHAPTER 3

House guests should never arrive bearing ill tidings

Yarborough Manor, the Duke of Hetherington's country estate

Feeling more stunned than shaken, Evie said, "Whatever happened out there had nothing to do with the sun hitting your eyes."

Tom turned slightly. His blue eyes, made more intense by dark lashes, lifted, the visor from his chauffeur's cap casting a slight shadow over them.

After a moment, he murmured, "I don't wish to

alarm you, ma'am. But I think it would be a good idea if I stayed here instead of at the pub."

Trying to settle her thoughts as well as her thumping heart, Evie murmured, "We'll talk about it later." She wanted to say guests did not arrive at the Duke of Heatherington's manor house in a state of panic but held her tongue for fear that she might entice him to break with protocol and damn propriety to hell and back.

She couldn't say for sure, but something told her Tom Winchester would set aside his role as the Countess of Woodridge's chauffeur and show his true colors if pushed too far. She knew her granny had entertained a secret agenda when she'd suggested employing Tom as her driver and Evie had even suspected him of serving a role far beyond that of chauffeur.

Bodyguard came to mind.

After all, she had already inherited two fortunes and stood to inherited several more.

She watched him lower his eyes and take a deep swallow. Oh, yes, Evie thought. Guarded and well-contained. When he lifted his gaze toward her again, she gave a stiff nod. "Actually, wait around. I will send Caro down with a message." That should give her enough time to settle the events in her mind. She really didn't wish to go into hysterics over something that might have been an accident or a silly prank, nor could she dismiss it as inconsequential.

"Yes, ma'am."

When Tom emerged from the vehicle and held the door open for her, Evie hesitated for a moment.

Something had happened on the road. She hadn't heard a gunshot, but if someone had fired from a distance, she might not have heard it.

She looked toward the entrance and saw the butler and a footman waiting at attention.

The importance of adhering to protocol had been drummed into her well before she'd set sail for England all those years ago as a bright-eyed debutante. Set a foot wrong and news about it would spread like wildfire.

How could she raise the alarm when she didn't know exactly what had happened?

Tom certainly knew more than he wanted to say. Giving another firm nod, she decided she would talk to him later… after she'd had a talk with her host.

Evie fixed her smile in place and strode toward the entrance just as the Duke of Hetherington, Bicky to his close friends, emerged, all smiles and good cheer.

"Evie, my darling. How absolutely marvelous it is to see you after such a long time. How long has it been?"

"Too long, Bicky. I have missed you."

The Duke of Hetherington turned to his butler. "Larkin. Please see to the Countess's luggage."

The butler bowed his head. "As you wish, Your Grace."

Evie glanced back at Tom and found him staring at her.

"Are you all right?" Bicky asked.

"Y-yes." Evie held her hand to her chest. She needed a moment to settle more than her thoughts.

Stepping inside Yarborough Manor had always given Evie a sense of the grand scale the so-called cottages back home in Newport aspired to emulate.

Massive columns flanked the entrance with the marble floors spreading all the way to the grand staircase that led to rooms fit for royalty. The sumptuous ballroom with its sparkling chandeliers and priceless works of art as well as the dining room were to the right and the library, billiards room and various sitting rooms and drawing rooms were situated at the opposite end.

Evie knew the house had been a gift from a monarch given in gratitude for a battle won in the 1500s. Along with the house, there had also been the creation of the title. These days, she thought, someone would be lucky to get a medal for valor.

"I suppose you'll want to settle in," Bicky said in his jovial manner.

"Yes, even with a new car, the drive over didn't feel any shorter. I know I could have traveled by train, but I knew I'd want to stop along the way to pick up a few essentials and the scenery is something I had looked forward to enjoying."

"When you're ready, join me in the blue drawing room," Bicky invited.

The butler cleared his throat and led the way up the grand staircase.

Evie strode up, removing her gloves, one finger at a time while her eyes wandered over to the tapestries and paintings adorning the walls.

She silently smiled as she recalled her mother's remark when she had traveled to England for Evie's wedding.

So much of everything. Where does it all come from?

"Thank you, Larkin." As she strode into her elegantly appointed room decorated in various shades of blue, the butler closed the door, leaving Evie alone.

She stopped in the middle of the room and sighed. It almost felt like coming home. She supposed it all had to do with the fond memories she had created when she'd first visited.

Setting her gloves down, she looked at her hands. They were shaking. She strode to the window and gazed out across the perfectly manicured lawns. "What on earth could have happened out there?"

She'd have to find the appropriate moment to mention it to Bicky, if anything, to alert him to the possible presence of poachers in the area. Her mind simply refused to consider any other explanation.

She replayed the moment in her mind and it still didn't make sense. Tom had claimed the sun had hit his eyes, but Evie knew that had not been the case because the sun had been almost above them.

Hearing the door open, she turned. "Ah, Caro. I see you made it in one piece."

Her lady's maid rushed in, her cheeks slightly tinged with a hint of pink. "Milady. Tom said to keep a close eye on you but he didn't explain. Then, he drove off like a bat out of hell... Has something happened?"

"No need to worry, Caro." Despite still feeling shaken up, Evie gave an insouciant shrug. "Nothing but a slight mishap on our way over here." She hoped Tom didn't prove her wrong. Had he gone back to search the area?

She should have mentioned it to Bicky...

"Are you sure?" Caro asked as she turned and signaled to the footman who had followed her in to set the luggage down at the bottom of the canopied bed.

Evie pointed to a small case. "Do that one first, please. I need to change out of these traveling clothes. Also, I'm about to write a brief note which I'd like you to take down to Tom." Assuming he would come back.

Evie settled down at the desk and set her mind to composing clear instructions for Tom, suggesting the pub would be the ideal place to hear of any news.

Drawing in a calming breath, Evie asked, "By the way, how was your visit? Are your parents well?"

"Yes, milady. Thank you for asking. They send their regards. I had a lovely break. The whole family gathered for a dinner last night to send me off again."

At one time, Caro had been employed by the Duke's household and she had taken care of Lady Constance, the Duke's younger sister.

When Evie had first visited all those years ago, she had arrived without a lady's maid and Caro had stepped in to assist her. Then, after the war, Lady Constance had been taken by the Spanish flu, leaving Caro without a position in the household. Something Evie had been only too happy to help with.

Evie sighed. It all seemed like an eternity ago. Yet, only a few years had elapsed. So much had happened since the war.

"Did you manage well without me, milady?"

Evie smiled. Caro had traveled with her to America. When they had returned two months before, Evie had given her a vacation to visit her family. "You're irreplaceable, Caro. Millicent did her best to step into your shoes, but you know how she tends to prattle on about her beaus. I have a good mind to send her to granny. I think they would get on well together."

"Oh, yes. Millicent would love that, milady. She's forever going on about wanting to travel and live in the Wild West."

"Yes, well…as you know, Newport is not exactly the Wild West." Evie finished writing her note to Tom, slipped it inside an envelope and handed it to Caro.

Fifteen minutes later, Caro returned. "I don't mean to get Tom into trouble, milady."

"Go on," Evie encouraged. She expected Caro to say he hadn't returned and had been quite prepared to make an excuse for him.

"Well, he was none too pleased when he read your message. I could tell by the way his jaw muscles clenched."

Evie had no trouble imagining his response. He had appeared stubbornly determined to remain at the house. However, Evie had the feeling he would serve a better purpose at the pub; the hub of village gossip.

"Caro? Has there been any shooting these last few days on the estate?"

"Not that I know of. In fact, the gentlemen have been complaining of boredom."

So, the others had arrived early too. "Who else is here?"

Caro laid out a set of brushes on the dresser and looked up in thought. "Well, there's Viscount Maison. His father has been complaining of ill health so the Viscount is doing what he can to sow his wild oats before taking on the responsibilities of the estate. Lord Chambers and his wife, Lady Charlotte arrived earlier with Mr. Mark Harper. Of course, Lady Porteus is here."

"Ah, good. It's been too long since I last saw the Duke's sister." Elizabeth had taken her sister's passing very hard and had gone into deep mourning for much longer than required. However, love had conquered the day and she had married an untitled landowner. As a duke's daughter, however, she retained the right to be addressed as Lady.

Caro continued running through her attendance list, "Lady Hammond is also here."

"Is Penelope here with her husband?" Evie asked. She had recently seen Lord Hammond in town. Although, she couldn't recall exactly where she had seen him. Evie shifted and frowned. Or had she actually seen Penelope? Hard to say, she thought. The moment she set foot outside her house, she saw so many people, she sometimes struggled to keep up.

"No, milady. According to Lady Penelope's maid, Lord Hammond had business to attend to and couldn't make it. Something to do with the estate. She's being her usual quiet self. I'm surprised I got that much information out of her." Caro clicked her fingers. "Lady Gloriana is also attending the house party. Although, she is staying with the Dowager Duchess."

Evie smiled. Bicky's cousin never missed a single event and she always made sure to take every opportunity she could get to ingratiate herself with the Dowager. "I suppose she's still hoping to inherit the Dowager's pearls." Evie tilted her head. "What about the Duchess?" Not her favorite person, Evie thought, but it would sound odd if she didn't ask about her.

Caro seemed to hesitate. "Word downstairs is that she is running late and will join the party tomorrow."

"Oh, where is she?"

Caro again hesitated. "London, milady. I heard something about some last-minute fittings for her new wardrobe."

That gave her another day to prepare. At one time, before either one had married, Bicky's wife had been Evie's fiercest competitor in the marriage stakes and had made no bones about showing her claws.

"If my count is correct, and to quote Elizabeth Bennet, that's too many ladies and not enough gentleman." Seeing Caro's eyes brighten, Evie added, "Not that I mind. It's all the same to me." Everyone had expected her to land a new husband within the year. There had been offers. None she could take seriously. In her opinion, some people could not be replaced.

"How is everyone getting on downstairs?" Evie asked.

"They're all finding their way around. Of course, it's easy for me, what with me having worked at Yarborough Manor."

"Of course." Evie winked at her maid. "Anyone interesting? Perhaps one of the chauffeurs?"

"There are only two and they're too old for me."

"Only two. How did the others get here?"

"Lady Gloriana and Lady Elizabeth traveled together. Lady Penelope traveled by train but then she didn't have far to travel from Lancashire. The others came by train too."

Caro stood behind her and inspected her hair. "I see Millicent has been taking good care of you during my absence, milady."

"She's a quick learner, we have to give her that." Evie turned slightly. "Now, what have you brought out for me to wear?"

As she slipped into her pale green skirt, Evie studied Caro who seemed intent on making sure everything fitted perfectly. "Caro. I get the feeling there is something you are not telling me. Out with it."

"Well... You know I'm not one to gossip."

Evie rolled her eyes. "And you know you are to keep me well informed. How else am I supposed to avoid making a faux pas or, if need be, reparation?"

"It's the Duchess... and the Duke. I hear they've been having quite a few spats of late."

"Really? What about?"

"It's not really my place to say." Caro looked over her shoulder as if she expected someone to be within hearing. She leaned in and whispered, "Infidelity, milady."

CHAPTER 4

Emily Post: The only time one can interrupt in the middle of a sentence is when you need to communicate something that honestly can't wait.

The Blue Drawing Room, Yarborough Manor

𝒰nlike wine, bad news did not improve with time...

Calling on her patience, Evie glanced around the blue drawing room. She needed to find the right moment to speak with Bicky. The butler had told her

Bicky would be along shortly but that had been half an hour ago.

She would have to speak with him in private or risk sending everyone into a state of panic.

Would he welcome news about trouble when he had other concerns to deal with? Nonsense, she thought. Of course, this would concern him. It had taken place on his estate which stretched for miles in any direction.

She wished Tom had been more forthcoming with his suspicions, if he had any. Although, he probably knew as much as she did. According to Caro, when she'd taken the note down to Tom, she'd had to wait for him because he had left. Evie assumed he had returned to see if he could find anything out on the road. If he had found anything, he hadn't mentioned it to Caro.

"You've been in town all this time and you didn't contact us?" Lady Chambers, Charlotte to her friends, emphasized her displeasure by taking a quick sip of her tea. "Unforgivable. Think of all the lunches we might have enjoyed."

Yes, Evie had been fully aware of what she'd been missing out on, hence her decision to spare herself the agony.

Charlotte's conversations tended to start off on the right foot. Inevitably, she then steered them in the opposite direction, always indulging in her pet hobby by setting her target on some poor unfortunate debutante and tearing her reputation to shreds.

Bicky strode in and clapped his hands. "We're all here." He looked around the room. "Well, most of us are. I suppose they'll be coming along soon." Seeing Evie sitting by the fireplace, he smiled. "Evie. Larkin tells me you blazed along the driveway in a new motor car. I'm afraid I missed your grand entrance. I know the car would have been right in front of me, but I only had eyes for you."

"I don't know what came over my chauffeur," Evie said, and she couldn't wait to have a proper word with him. Now that she thought about it, she'd swear Tom had been trying to get her to safety.

Charles, Viscount Maison, lifted his cup in a salute. "I actually saw it drive away. Very flashy. Is it new?"

Like all men of his generation, the Viscount enjoyed talking about motor vehicles and all things mechanical. "We brought it over with us from America. It's a *Duesenberg*."

Matthew, Lord Chambers, sat opposite Evie and gave a nod of approval. "It only just came out. Someone mentioned it at the club. Very impressive." He clicked his fingers. "I heard someone refer to it as a *duesy*."

It certainly was an outstanding piece of machinery. Although, she would still credit Tom for the smooth drive.

Matthew's wife, Charlotte, sighed. "He's been going

on and on about getting a new motor car. I honestly don't see what's wrong with the one we have. It's comfortable enough and should see us through to our old age."

Matthew Chambers snorted. "I believe my mother said those precise words when father presented her with a new horse drawn carriage back in 1890. Now she's speeding through the countryside in her Rolls." Looking at Evie, he said, "I hope it came to no harm during the crossing."

Evie gave him a distracted smile. "Not even a scratch, or so I'm told. We had calm seas all the way."

She saw the butler approach Bicky and murmur in his ear. Bicky nodded and followed the butler out of the drawing room.

Charlotte leaned in slightly. "Lovely ensemble. Paris?"

Evie gave a small nod. "By way of New York." It had taken some doing, but she had managed to place an order with her modiste.

Fashionable ladies made a couple of annual pilgrimages to the capital of fashion. During the months of March and September, droves of women were seen entering the Parisian studios of famous designers. The lucky few, had their own personal assistant to help with the selection of their wardrobe for the coming season. Some viewed the activity as an absolute must in order to outshine both their friends and enemies. Evie enjoyed her new gowns, but there always seemed to be something else to think about.

Bicky returned and went to stand by a window.

Excusing herself, Evie strode across the room to join him.

"You're being unusually quiet," Evie remarked. "Is this a new trend with you?"

Bicky instantly brightened. "Oh, I seem to have lapsed into some sort of inner musing. It happens sometimes. My father would be proud. He never really held high expectations for me, always complaining I didn't give much thought to anything."

"It's not as if you do have much to think about now that everything has been sorted out for you." The old Duke had been instrumental in carrying the family forward through to the new century, introducing all the modern conveniences of the time. This had been quite a feat for someone of his generation; an Edwardian through and through. In the process, he had nearly sent the family bankrupt, hence Bicky's eventual marriage to an heiress.

"I hear Clara is away." As a dear old friend, she wouldn't want him to suffer in silence. She knew Clara could be exacting in her manner and Bicky often came across as a *bon vivant*. Even so, he would be the last man to break his vows.

He gave her a tight smile. "The usual, I'm afraid. You

know Clara loves her new gowns. It's all become quite a compulsion."

With gowns or with something or someone else? Evie wouldn't press him for more. Unlike her love match, she knew his had been a marriage of convenience. A much-coveted title for Clara in exchange for hard cold cash to rescue the estate from ruin for Bicky.

She cleared her throat and prompted herself to ask about poachers in the area when Mark Harper strode in and beamed at Evie.

As heir to his cousin, the Earl of Chatterlain, he received invitations everywhere, especially to households with marriageable daughters. It came as no surprise to see him here where he knew he would be safe for a few days, at least...

"I'd heard a rumor you were back. I don't understand why Bicky kept your visit a secret," Mark said. "But here you are. What happened? What brought you back?"

"Some would say prohibition happened." Evie smiled at him. "I'm afraid it's nothing more than the call of duty. As custodian of the Woodridge estate I must, on occasion, put in an appearance. As much as I wanted to extend my stay, I had to face up to responsibilities."

"Prohibition." Matthew visibly shivered. "What do you do for pre-dinner drinks?"

Evie laughed. "We reminisce."

Charlotte raised her teacup in a salute. "To think, a well-organized group of women brought it all about."

"Have some more cake, dear," Matthew offered as he shared a knowing smile with Evie. "You're always raving about the Duke's brandy fruitcake."

"Oh, yes. Thank you."

Evie once again turned to Bicky but before she could say anything, Lady Penelope and Lady Elizabeth arrived together, all full of greetings and questions about Evie's voyage.

"Are we the last to arrive?" Bicky's sister, Elizabeth, asked.

Before anyone could answer, the butler made his announcement because the lady in question wouldn't have it any other way.

"Lady Gloriana."

Lady Gloriana Aspendale, the Duke's cousin and married to the youngest son of an Earl, entered and launched into a diatribe about the Dowager Duchess' fickle manner, a subject enjoyed by Lady Charlotte, so the two women sat together and swapped anecdotal proof of the Dowager's capricious manner.

Bicky laughed. "At least, mama's opinion never wavers where I'm concerned. I've always been her favorite son."

Little did he know…

Evie shook her head. It wouldn't do to rob him of his illusions. "Bicky. There's something I've been meaning to tell you." Evie turned to set her cup and saucer down.

Her natural inclination would be to blurt out the news but she understood this required delicate handling. After all, the Duke had a duty to oversee his lands and ensure the safety of all who dwelt within it. If anything went wrong, he would see it as a personal affront.

In the next instant, she heard an odd sound. Like a champagne cork popping, she thought. Turning, her eyes widened.

Bicky looked as though he'd just seen a ghost.

His face paled. He swayed and finally, his legs gave way and he buckled down to the ground.

CHAPTER 5

Who will inherit?

The Duke of Hetherington's bedchamber

"*I*t's nothing," Bicky insisted, his voice carrying an uncharacteristic streak of stubbornness. "Stop fussing."

"Your Grace. The wound could become infected," Dr. Higgins, the village medical practitioner explained. "We need to bandage it properly."

"Nonsense. I have guests," Bicky complained.

"And they will understand," Dr. Higgins assured him.

Evie, accompanied by the Duke's sister, Elizabeth, pushed past the butler and, ignoring his raised eyebrows, entered Bicky's room.

Wringing her hands together, Evie asked. "Will he be all right?" Somehow, she felt responsible.

Protocol, propriety... manners. Honestly, everything she'd imagined Tom damning to hell and back had conspired against her. For once, she should have behaved like the brash American everyone assumed her to be. If she had, then Bicky would have been spared...

"It's only a superficial wound." Dr. Higgins turned to Bicky. "I'm afraid it will be quite sore for a few days. Your Grace, I suggest you refrain from shooting for a while."

Until that moment, Lady Elizabeth had looked quite pale. However, hearing the doctor's instructions, she gave an unladylike snort. "I doubt my brother will heed your advice."

Bicky stuck his chin out. "Indeed, I will not. I survived the Battle of the Somme, this is nothing but an inconvenience." Bicky looked up. "Larkin will look after me. Where's Stevens?"

The valet stepped forward. "Right here, Your Grace."

"You'll be able to fashion some sort of contraption for me, won't you, Stevens?"

"Certainly, Your Grace."

Bicky held his injured arm up. "Forget I said that. I think I'll manage to dress properly for dinner. I wouldn't have it any other way." He watched the doctor at work for a moment and then said, "Larkin."

The butler stepped forward. "Your Grace?"

"Tell cook to cut my food into small portions. Tonight, I will be a one-handed man."

"Your Grace. You really should rest," Dr. Higgins urged.

"And yet, I insist. I refuse to be brought down by a mere flesh wound." Turning to Larkin, he asked, "Have the police been informed?"

The butler nodded. "The steward has organized his men to search the grounds. I believe the groundskeeper and stable hands have joined in the search."

"Well, that's a start." Bicky tried to sit up but Dr. Higgins placed a staying hand on his good arm.

"Oh, good heavens, man," Bicky complained, "I should at least be allowed to sit up in my own bed."

"Bicky," his sister urged. "You got your way and you'll be having dinner with your guests. Meanwhile, do as you are told, please."

"I suppose I should. Any idea what happened?" The Duke looked from one person to the other.

Evie leaned in and whispered, "If I could have a word with you."

Bicky appeared to struggle to understand her

meaning. Finally, with a wave of his uninjured hand, Bicky sent everyone out of the room, saying, "Elizabeth, please make sure our guests are well entertained."

"You seem to forget, I am a guest here too," Elizabeth replied, her face showing the relief she clearly felt at seeing her brother had survived the ordeal with only a minor scratch. "Of course, I'll do all I can."

The doctor left saying he would call in again in the morning.

"I'm not likely to die from a scratch," Bicky bellowed. "I've had worse from my valet when he shaved me after one of his drinking bouts." Bicky looked over at his valet and mouthed an apology.

When they were alone, he turned to Evie. "Are you going to reprimand me too?"

Evie smiled. "I should. I really should." She looked at the door to make sure it had been closed. "I've been meaning to tell you. Actually, I've been trying to find the right moment to tell you. On our way over, we had an incident on the road." She took in his shocked expression and gave him a nod of assurance. "I'm fine but… Well, I wonder if this is related." She wrung her hands together. "Maybe you've been experiencing problems with poachers on the estate…"

"What sort of incident did you have? And… Poachers?" He could not have sounded more affronted.

Evie told him what she knew, and wished she had more details to share.

Again, Bicky tried to sit up. "You think someone shot at you and then tried their luck with me?"

It all sounded too real when he said it. "Or they might have tried to run us off the road. I can't be sure. There might have been a gunshot. Perhaps they used a mirror to cast a reflection and blind my chauffeur."

"To what end?"

Trying to remain calm, she actually managed to downplay the seriousness of the matter. Evie gave a casual shrug. "Your guess is as good as mine. I wanted to think it had all been a dreadful mistake or a mishap of sorts but then, you were shot. Clearly, something is going on."

"Who stands to inherit?" Bicky shook his head. "I'm sorry to be blunt, but it is the first question anyone would ask."

"The real question being who would want to see me dead?" Evie asked, her eyebrows slightly curved. She held his gaze for a moment and then moved to stand by the window.

"You're right," Bicky said. "Two incidents in one day. There's nothing coincidental about that."

She couldn't help thinking they were all sitting ducks. If anything happened to her… "You know I have a brother but he is as rich as *Croesus*. He doesn't need my money. Besides, he loves me."

Bicky chortled. "What is it with you Americans?

You magnetize money and massive fortunes like bees to honey. It must be in your blood."

Taking the remark with the blitheness it had been intended, Evie said, "Perhaps we're more open to change and opportunity and... risks." Evie chuckled. "In any case, we don't exactly hold exclusive rights to wealth creation."

This time, Bicky snorted. "And yet, every American I've ever met..." he waved his hand. "I just heard myself. My apologies. Of course, I have only met a handful of your compatriots. But you must admit, they all have vast amounts of wealth in common and, clearly, more opportunities than they know what to do with."

Evie watched as a group of estate workers made their way across to the folly, their dogs running ahead of them. "I won't argue with that. However..."

Bicky laughed. "This is where you gently illustrate your point."

Evie shrugged. "I inherited and had nothing to do with creating my wealth. On the other hand, someone like Helena Rubinstein..."

Bicky tilted his head in thought. "The name rings a bell."

"She is the crowned queen of cosmetics, or at least, she shares the podium with Elizabeth Arden. In any case, she has claims to humble beginnings as an émigré to the new world, not America but rather Australia."

Shifting, she leaned in and looked out toward the other end of the estate where she saw another group of estate workers spreading out.

"Ah, the Antipodes. I have a distant cousin who settled in Australia and met the most wonderful woman. He mentioned the astonishing number of sheep they own and, to be honest, I still can't quite get my head around it." Bicky patted his arm. "In any case, this injury of mine must be affecting my head. Please continue with your story before I succumb to another bout of idiocy."

Evie smiled. "As a young Polish émigré in Australia, Helena Rubinstein saw the opportunity to produce face lotions. She set up a small business which, in no time, flourished and expanded. Then she swiftly established herself here and followed her success to America. We're merely reaping the rewards of her industrious endeavors. There are many like her who see an opportunity and grasp it with both hands, eventually making a brilliant success of it."

Studying the landscape from the window, Evie tapped a finger on her chin as she considered Bicky's earlier question.

She knew of one person who would stand to inherit something from her.

Seth Halton, the current Earl of Woodridge.

Her husband, Nicholas Halton, had died without issue. When the title had been created, provisions had been made for such an occasion to prevent the title from dying out so it had passed on to a distant relative. Unfortunately, he had been a casualty of the Great War. However, well before dying, he'd fathered a son; a young boy still in the schoolroom.

Not exactly the instigator of evil machinations, Evie thought.

As for her brother…

If anything were to happen to her, the bulk of her fortune would revert to her brother and he would, most likely, set up a foundation to assist some worthy cause.

Evie shook her head. "I can't believe someone would wish me ill." As for Bicky being shot…

Another impossibility. Everyone loved Bicky.

Bicky huffed out a breath. "Well, before you told me about your incident on the road, I had begun to wonder if someone wanted me dead."

Evie turned to look at him.

Had Clara…?

No. Impossible.

The Duchess would never stoop so low or take such a foolish risk. Evie knew for a fact she had a penchant for diamonds hanging around her neck. Not a noose.

Frowning, she wondered why she had even thought about Bicky's wife. Drawing in a deep breath, she remembered.

Caro had told her she'd heard talk of infidelity.

Giving a small nod, Bicky said, "You have to admit, the circumstances are rather odd. We were both standing by the window. Either one of us could have been the target, but you'd already had an attempt on your life."

"We don't really know that for sure."

Bicky shook his head and winced, "I don't mean to frighten you, but let's assume there has been an attempt…"

Evie thought back to that precise moment when she'd heard the popping sound. She had only seconds before shifted to set her cup and saucer down. Had she been the target all along?

Evie struggled to accept the day's events. It all seemed too incredulous. Although, the fact remained, someone had made an attempt on someone's life.

Not once, but twice.

"It might only have been a warning," she mused. However, she feared they wouldn't know for sure until the perpetrator was caught.

A thick silence settled between them.

Evie knew she'd made a few enemies along the way, but none who'd be prepared to risk their freedom or even be the type who would snub her in public. But she had made enemies.

What could they gain? To get her out of the way? She didn't pose a threat. Not anymore. Evie had made it plainly clear to anyone who would listen. She would never marry again.

Frowning, she wondered where the thought had come from. There seemed to be far too many assailing her mind. She supposed the thought had been there since she'd made the decision to return to England. Then, there had been her granny's warning about being perceived as a threat.

Ah, but what if this had to do with some sort of belated reprisal for her first marriage? Her granny had warned her about the possibility of that happening.

Nicholas had been a catch.

His estates were not entailed. If they'd had a daughter, the title would have gone to her, along with all the property. As it was, the title had transferred to the next of kin, but the property and wealth had remained in Evie's control.

Of course, she would do her utmost to ensure the estate remained intact. The current Earl would not come into possession until he came of age. Meanwhile, she remained responsible for his wellbeing. The young boy had not only lost his father but soon after, his mother had succumbed to ill health, possibly brought on by the premature death of her husband.

She received regular reports of the child's welfare. Had someone new come into Seth's life? Perhaps someone keen to influence the child?

If anything happened to her...

No. She simply refused to think about it. Nevertheless, she made a mental note to contact Seth's guardian and make sure nothing unusual had been happening in his life.

Bicky broke the silence and asked, "Are we going to let the others know?"

Evie shook her head. "I'm not sure that's a good idea. Besides, what would you tell them? That someone wants you dead or maybe they want me dead?" Could she trust them to keep the information to themselves? She wanted to think so, but the rumor mills had a way of cranking up and word spreading faster than the industrial revolution.

"What does your chauffeur say about all this? After all, he was a witness to the first incident."

"I'm not sure yet. I insisted he stay at the pub." Evie didn't want to explain her reasons for doing that for fear of appearing to cast aspersions on Bicky's household. "I suppose I should move away from the window. Although, I imagine we should be safe now. You have all your people running about the place. That's enough to scare anyone off." She looked out across the gardens. "It's strange. You don't have many trees near the house. One would think those ones near the folly would be too far away to use as a camouflage."

"Not necessarily," Bicky disagreed. "Some rifles are quite efficient from a great distance."

"Yes, I suppose you'd know all about that."

Bicky plumped up his pillow with his good hand. "The Whitworth," he mused.

"What's that?"

"A single shot rifle. It has been in use since the 1850s. You should know something about it since it was used by Confederate sharpshooters in the American Civil War claiming the lives of several Union generals. It possesses excellent long-range accuracy. I believe we have a couple in our collection."

Evie checked the clock on the mantle. If she wanted to meet with Tom, she would have to set off now so she could be back in time to dress for dinner. Of course, she could telephone him and ask him to meet her here. After all, he had the car.

At the sound of a knock at the door, Bicky answered with a sharp, "Come in."

"My apologies for disturbing you, Your Grace."

"Yes, what is it, Larkin?"

"Miss Clarissa Wainscot has just ridden in. Should I show her through to the blue drawing room?"

"Miss who?" Bicky asked.

"Lady Wainscot's daughter, Your Grace."

"What the devil is she doing here?"

Larkin slanted his gaze toward Evie. "Miss Wainscot inquired after Lady Woodridge, Your Grace."

Bicky turned to Evie who shrugged.

Larkin cleared his throat. "Begging your pardon, Your Grace. I believe Miss Wainscot is after some news. I also believe Lady Wainscot might have sent her… as a scout."

Evie scratched around her mind trying to place the lady in question but came up empty.

"She's a neighbor," Bicky explained. "Lives out at Hainsley Hall. Married to Baron Wainscot. He's a good sort but the wife…" Bicky cringed. "She has two unmarried daughters. Need I say more?"

No, he needn't bother.

Mamas with daughters of marriageable ages were notorious for drawing their claws during the process of carrying out their maternal duties to their offspring.

"I'll go down," Evie offered.

"No need to bother," Bicky said. "The others can entertain her."

The butler gave a stiff nod. "Very well, Your Grace. I shall convey the message as best I can."

"I suppose I'm about to become the talk of the county," Evie mused. "It can't be helped. The locals were bound to be curious about my return." Although, she still couldn't imagine why that should be.

"What if it's more than that?" Bicky asked.

"What do you mean?"

"Surely you must have heard the rumors when you first married Nicholas. You snatched him right from under all those mamas' noses. Until you came along, he'd been the most eligible bachelor around."

"Oddly enough, I only just entertained the same

thought." Evie tried to find some humor in it. "Do you think I'm about to get some belated backlash for stealing him away?"

"It's quite possible. People might think you're here to fish around for your next husband. You've done it once. What's to stop you from doing it again?"

Evie threw her head back and laughed. "If that had been my intention, I would have stayed in town. London always has the most promising candidates and opportunities."

"You seem to forget we have Mark Harper staying. Heir to his cousin, the Earl of Chatterlain. Not to mention Charles, Viscount Maison and also heir to his father's title."

Oh, yes... She had forgotten.

"The more I think about it, the more convinced I become... Oh, never mind." She couldn't be the target. Surely not...

CHAPTER 6

An unexpected visitor

The Blue Drawing Room

*P*romising to bring back some news, Evie returned to the drawing room where she found Miss Clarissa Wainscot deep in conversation with Lady Charlotte.

Glancing around the drawing room, Evie received several nods. Clearly, Elizabeth had provided them with an update on Bicky's condition. While everyone appeared to be eager for more news, they knew better than to bring up the subject in front of a visitor.

Dressed in riding clothes, Miss Clarissa's manner came across as exuberant. She sat on the edge of her chair, looking ready to jump into action at a moment's notice.

It took a moment for Evie to actually place the young woman. When she did, she realized she had actually heard of her two years before.

Little did Miss Clarissa know Charlotte, Lady Chambers, had already made sport of her, declaring the fact the young Miss had reached the ripe old age of twenty-three without a single proposal as a veritable catastrophe. The girl had become a pariah for no other reason than her failure to shackle a man. Any man. It stood to reason, there had to be something wrong with her. Now, at twenty-five, Evie imagined Charlotte had cast the young girl as an absolutely lost cause.

To Evie's surprise, Charlotte appeared to have had some sort of change of heart.

As Evie strode in, Charlotte chirped, "You'll never guess, so I'll tell you. I have just agreed to sponsor Miss Wainscot in the coming season. She shall be my guest when I next visit town."

Evie couldn't tell if Charlotte had made a sincere offer or if she'd merely wished to distract Miss Wainscot with a bee's knees type of promise which she might or might not keep.

"Splendid," Evie offered and strode across the room.

However, the small distance she had tried to put between herself and Miss Wainscot did not deter the young Miss.

"Lady Woodridge. Are you here for the weekend or will you stay longer?" Miss Wainscot asked, which seemed rather forward since they hadn't even been properly introduced.

Before Evie could deliver her reply, Charlotte, bless her heart, piped in, "We'll have to sort out your wardrove for your upcoming season. Competition is very stiff. Of course, I can't promise anything, but I'm sure I can secure invitations to the sort of affairs where we might catch a glimpse of the Prince of Wales."

Miss Wainscot gasped. "The Prince of Wales! Mama will be beside herself when I tell her."

Charlotte gave a knowing nod. "Then you should make haste. I'm sure you're simply dying to share the news with your mama."

Miss Wainscot rose to her feet only to waver. After all, she had presumably received clear instructions from her mama to extricate as much information as she could. It stood to reason, she could not return to Hainsley Hall empty-handed.

At any other time, Evie would have humored the young woman with a tidbit, something… anything to take back with her, but she didn't feel inclined to be generous. Not when she had an injured Duke and a possible attempt or two on her life to contend with.

Nevertheless... She forced herself to dig deep.

"It just occurred to me," Evie said, "I made an appointment at *Marceline's Salon de Beaute* without taking into account the planned activities at Yarborough Manor. Would you do me the favor of taking my place for a day of beauty treatment tomorrow? I'm sure the proprietress won't mind," she offered the young woman. "You want to be at your best when you're... presented to the Prince of Wales."

Miss Wainscot gasped again. It seemed all her Christmases were coming at once. "You would do that... for me?" She turned to Charlotte and then back to Evie, her lips still slightly parted. "I'd been reluctant to impose on His Grace, but I'm so glad I made the trip out here."

Finally, Evie thought, as Miss Wainscot made a move to leave.

She couldn't help pondering over the effort it had taken to eject the young woman from the manor house without injuring her pride. In their place, anyone else would have simply shown her the door.

Larkin cleared his throat the way he did when he was ready to announce someone.

Good heavens, Evie thought. What now? Or, rather... Who?

"There is a gentleman inquiring after Lady Woodridge. A Mr. Winchester."

It took a moment for Evie to realize he meant Tom. What on earth had possessed her chauffeur to come here and request an audience with her and why had he introduced himself as Mr. Winchester?

Evie glanced over at Miss Wainscot and could see her ears had pricked up.

Larkin cleared his throat again. "I'm sure His Grace will not mind if I show the gentleman to the library."

Nodding, Evie hoped he would be swift about it so Miss Wainscot would not cross paths with Mr. Winchester.

However, Miss Wainscot had other ideas and, appearing to remember her priorities, she scurried after the butler saying, "Oh, Larkin. You could show me out first. That way you won't have to make a round trip."

"As you wish, Miss Clarissa."

Charlotte rolled her eyes and sunk back into her chair mouthing, "I tried."

"Yes, thank you." Evie hesitated, however she went on to say, "I am indebted to you." She didn't want to be, but a lack of gratitude would be a black mark against her. "I simply don't understand why there is so much interest in my visit to Yarborough."

It seemed Evie had been living in a state of blissful ignorance because everyone's eyebrows quirked up.

As Bicky had wickedly pointed out, she was in the presence of two eligible bachelors.

"*Argh*! I feel as though I'm caught in a spider's web and possibly one of my own making because I've been protesting too much." No, she would not marry again.

Her widened eyes jumped from Charles, Viscount Maison to Mark Harper who both grinned and winked at her. "Stop it. At once!"

"But think of the sport we could have," Charles said.

She didn't know Mark Harper very well, and yet, he played along too.

"We might end up with an epic and outmoded pistols at dawn battle for you, Countess. Even if we don't, think of how much fun it would be to spread the rumor about."

Evie recovered and gave them both an impish smile. "Is that so? Well, I'm not greedy and I do enjoy a bit of sport as much as the next person. In fact, probably more so. I do like an even playing field so I might invite Miss Clarissa. I hear she has a sister and a very eager mama."

CHAPTER 7

Have we met?

$\mathcal{E}$vie strode into the library and found Mr. Winchester standing by the window, his hands in his pockets, his attention fixed on some faraway place.

"Tom," Evie whispered.

When he turned, she barely recognized him.

Tom had changed out of his chauffeur's uniform and into a soft collared shirt with a demure forest green tie and a fashionable two button suit jacket in earthy tones.

A tall man with broad shoulders and narrow hips,

he did the suit justice. In fact, she would easily mistake him for a country squire.

He strode up to her, his manner casual yet brisk and commanding.

"Ma'am. I hope you don't find me impertinent. I heard about the commotion at the house."

Word had spread? Already?

"By the way, I received your note and I can see the advantage of staying at the pub. In the brief time I was there, I heard enough conversations to realize how quickly word gets around. It would definitely serve as a vantage point. However…"

Evie nodded. "Things have changed." She gave him a brief summary of the events leading up to the shooting. "This time, there is no doubt. Someone took a shot at… Well, I don't know. So, I suppose there is still some sort of doubt."

"How is the Duke?" Tom asked.

"He's fine. He only suffered a flesh wound. Thank heavens. But it could have been worse. In fact, it could have been fatal. If I hadn't moved…" Evie pressed her hand to her throat. "I think I'm having a delayed reaction to the shock."

Tom gestured for her to sit down.

"Yes, I think I will."

He took the seat opposite her.

"By the way, how did you get here so fast?" Evie asked.

"I drove."

"And no one noticed you drove the car I'd arrived in?"

He shrugged. "Actually, I acquired a new car."

Evie's eyebrows curved upward, curiosity getting the better of her. She wondered how much effort she would have to employ to get Tom to share more details and expand his vocabulary from his usual mono-syllables.

Although…

He'd already said far more than he had in the two months he'd been working for her.

"A roadster," he explained.

Evie couldn't hide her surprise. "How did you manage that?"

He gave her a small smile. "I made an offer to a local man."

Anyone she knew? Evie couldn't help wondering.

"Sir Bradford. He's new to the area. When I arrived at the pub, he'd just settled down for a drink and engaged me in conversation about cars. As it turns out, he has quite a collection. Later, when I heard about the incident at the house, I approached him and… we made a deal." He shifted in his seat. "I thought it might be best if I came incognito."

The fact he had delivered such a lengthy explana-tion left her stunned. Recovering, Evie realized her chauffeur seemed to possess some interesting skills.

Her granny had mentioned something about Tom being in the war, but she had been short on details.

"At this point, ma'am, I would strongly advise against staying in this house."

Evie straightened and lifted her chin. "Nonsense. I will not be driven into hiding."

Tom pushed out a breath. "If you choose to stay on, I would advise against remaining alone."

"But I'm not alone, Tom."

"With all due respect, ma'am, I doubt your host is trained in such matters."

"Which matters?"

"Security, ma'am."

Evie's eyes widened again. "And you are?"

He held her gaze for a long moment. Evie had the feeling he might be weighing his words with great care and deciding what could be revealed and what needed to remain hidden.

Finally, he relented and said, "When your grand-mother sought out the services of a chauffeur, she had very particular requirements. They included the ability to look after your safety."

Evie gave him a small smile. "Are you by any chance referring to military skills?"

"Yes, ma'am."

"Well, rest assured, His Grace was an officer in the war. He fought in the Battle of the Somme and he survived."

Tom looked down and made an attempt to hide his smile.

"You're not impressed."

"On the contrary, ma'am. However, during the war, it would have been my job to look after officers such as His Grace."

To say she felt astonished over the revelation would be putting it mildly. Although, she had suspected Tom had been harboring some sort of secret past.

"Very well, Tom. What do you propose we do? I won't scurry away and hide like a scared rabbit."

He stood up and strode to the window. It seemed to be everyone's favorite place to gather their thoughts.

A few moments later, he declared, "I could be Mr. Winchester, a distant relative or a friend you encountered in London... You might have suggested calling on you here. No one would find that suspicious."

No, they wouldn't because, despite always trying her best to conform and adhere to the strictures of polite society, she couldn't avoid being true to herself, sometimes indulging in having her way and behaving like an eccentric.

Miraculously, she had never waltzed into anyone's drawing room with a trained pet monkey adorning her shoulder. Although, it had been a fantasy of hers since reading all about some ladies doing just that in the previous century when pet menageries had been all the rage.

Evie tossed the idea around.

Mr. Winchester. A distant relative.

Or... A friend, visiting London.

"We'll have to let the Duke in on the secret. I think he'll rather enjoy it." Evie shifted to the edge of her seat and tapped her chin in thought. "You're his height and... you'll need suitable clothes."

Tom looked pensive for a moment and then gave her an assuring nod. "I've already taken care of it."

Evie could barely hide her surprise. "I take it this person you met has been extremely accommodating." He looked puzzled, so she added, "Sir Bradford."

"Oh, him... Yes. He served during the war so we struck up an instant camaraderie."

"All right." Evie sat up. "How do we go about this exactly? Do we need to work on a story, something that will be credible to the others?"

"I suggest we try to stick as close as possible to the truth," he said.

And what would that be? Evie wondered, now more than ever feeling as though she knew next to nothing about Tom Winchester.

"If we are to be acquaintances, you could say your grandmother introduced us," he suggested. "Or perhaps... We could be childhood friends."

"How exactly would that work?" He looked to be at least three... maybe five years older... Yes, somewhere in his mid-thirties.

"It pays to be vague," he said. "We avoid specific dates and talk about instances that bring up relatable images. For instance, if anyone asks how old we'd been when we first met, I could pretend I'm giving it some thought and finally say, I remember teaching you to skate or swim."

"Really? Well… yes, I suppose that could work. Fine. We are long-time friends." Evie agreed with a nod and turned her thoughts to practicalities. "Larkin will need to be informed about the extra guest at the table. First, I will bring His Grace up to speed." Evie sat back and nibbled on the tip of her thumb.

She wished Bicky could come down for a moment.

Looking toward the library door, she wondered if Larkin had seen fit to hover nearby. If not, she could try to sneak Tom upstairs.

Reaching a decision, Evie gave a firm nod. "At my signal, follow me." She strode to the library door and eased it open a fraction. Peering out, she made sure the coast was clear. Seeing no one about, she signaled to Tom and they both hurried up the stairs.

"Actually, ma'am… It would be best if we simply pretend we're going about our business. If anyone sees us hurrying, they might suspect us of being up to no good."

True.

Evie murmured, "This is highly unusual, to say the least. But exhilarating."

They strode along the corridor at a more sedate pace. Evie prayed Bicky had been left alone to rest. She eased the door to his room open and whispered, "Bicky. It's me. I've brought someone with me."

It took some explaining but Bicky eventually came on board with the plan, agreeing with the idea of Tom joining the house party.

Tom said, "We'll need to hash out the details, Your Grace."

Bicky seemed to experience a momentary loss of attention, which he recovered by saying, "You are employed as the Countess's chauffeur and bodyguard."

Tom nodded.

When Bicky looked at Evie, she simply shrugged. "It's news to me too. Well, the latter part, at least." All along, she'd had a bodyguard. Had he followed her at a discreet distance when she'd stepped out for a stroll in the nearby parks?

"Do you believe there will be another attempt?" Bicky asked.

Tom set his mouth into a firm line. "I had a wander around the estate. No one stopped me. In fact, I didn't see anyone about. If someone is determined to get results, there is nothing to impede them."

"All right. I suppose I should ring for Larkin and let him know there will be an extra guest for dinner... In fact, for the weekend. He shall have to prepare a room. Now, more than ever, I will insist on attending dinner."

As Bicky rang the bell, he murmured, "What an extraordinary turn of events."

CHAPTER 8

Is there a Mrs. Winchester?

Evie's bedchamber...

$\mathcal{A}$s Caro arranged her hair, trying her best to tame the mop of curls, Evie noticed her frowning. "Is something wrong, Caro?"

Her maid gave a small shake of her head only to then nod. "I might be wrong, but earlier, as I was coming along the corridor and making my way to your room, I thought I saw Tom down the opposite end... coming out of His Grace's room." She shook her head again. "I must have imagined it." Stepping back, Caro inspected her work.

The Devil is in the detail, Evie thought...

Tom had suggested they needed to prepare for the unexpected. He'd also recommended being as vague as possible. However, in this instance, Evie didn't think she would be able to get away with anything but the truth.

She knew she could trust Caro to be discreet. But would her maid understand and... play along?

Lines of distinction existed because they made everyone's life that much easier. Without boundaries and the accompanying rules, no one would know how to behave.

Rolling her eyes heavenward, she wondered if she had just heard echoes of her granny in her mind. To be fair to her grandmother, she had made several new adjustments to better fit into the new century. Overall, however, her heart remained true to the previous era.

If they were to make a success of this charade, she supposed Caro would need to be in on the secret too.

Evie cleared her throat. "Well, as a matter of fact..." Scooping in a breath, Evie gave Caro an abbreviated version of the events which had taken place since... Well, since she'd set off from America.

When she finished relating her story, Evie urged, "Caro, you'll need to blink and breathe."

"Oh... Oh, my. I'm speechless. I mean, everyone

downstairs has been buzzing with the news about the shooting but now you say Tom has taken command of the situation because your grandmother secretly hired him as your personal bodyguard."

"That's about the gist of it," Evie agreed and stood up to inspect her reflection in the mirror, smiling as she cast an appreciative glance over her silk and satin evening gown.

She had abandoned her favorite shade of pale green for a rich shade of dazzling bronze with black beading and black embroidery. Admiring the column of sheer elegance, Evie turned and looked over her shoulder to study the effect of the low-cut V shape.

Having one's back to someone in a crowded room was never an excuse to skimp and the designer had done a splendid job, highlighting the edges with an intricate diamond shaped pattern made from black beads sewn into the satin trim.

Resuming her seat at the dressing table, she watched Caro select a necklace. She held it against Evie's neck so Evie could decide if she liked it or not.

"Yes, that will do." When the long strand of black pearls fell into place, Evie tilted her head and watched Caro pin a *diamante* dragonfly brooch. Deciding she already had enough adornments, she selected a small black feather for her hair attached to a narrow headband.

With a gentle dab of perfume on her wrists, Evie

rose to her feet and turned her attention to slipping her long gloves on.

When she heard a light knock at her door, Evie said, "That'll be him."

"Him? You mean, Tom. Here… in your room?"

Evie tried to play down the situation which, under any other circumstance, would have been deemed scandalous. "We needed to rendezvous for a…" She tried to recall the term Tom had used. "Oh, yes. A briefing session. He will be joining us for dinner and, as you can imagine, there are certain expectations. Rules to adhere to. If he is to remain incognito, Tom will need to play the role of gentleman to the hilt. He cannot put a foot wrong."

Caro blinked rapidly.

"You should open the door now and let him in before someone catches him hovering outside my room."

"Yes, milady." Caro hurried to the door and, grabbing hold of Tom's arm, pulled him inside only to then step back, her eyes wide, her expression beyond surprised.

"Well," Evie exclaimed. "You certainly clean up nicely."

Dressed in formal evening wear consisting of a black fitted jacket with long 'swallow' tails in the back, a white vest, trousers with silk stripes on the sides and a white bow tie, Tom Winchester had transformed himself from the country squire look she'd seen earlier to the picture-perfect image of a titled gentleman. A Sir, a Lord… A Viscount. Even the title of a Duke would suit him just fine, Evie thought.

"I take it I pass muster, ma'am."

Evie swallowed. "Yes, you most certainly do." It took some doing to tear her intrigued attention away from him. "Right… Well. Let's see." Evie drew in a long breath. "For starters, you mustn't call me ma'am."

His eyebrow lifted slightly.

Yes, she knew it would be a miracle if he managed to get through five minutes before reverting to old habits. After all, it had taken Evie more than two months to break him of the habit of calling her Lady Woodridge.

"Remind me again, are we to be related or did we decide on a long-standing friendship?" she asked, suddenly wondering which would be safest.

"Friends, I think," he said. "I know many of your family members, but I might be caught out. As friends, I can lay claim to knowing some of your immediate family. Your mother and grandmother as well as your brother."

"Yes, that makes sense," Evie agreed. "So… you must call me…"

"Evangeline."

Evie shook her head. "No, certainly not. My mother

always calls me that when I've landed myself into trouble."

The edge of his lip quirked up. "Evie."

"Try not to sound so surprised."

He tried it again. To his credit, it only took a dozen tries for Evie to claim satisfaction when, in fact, she had simply enjoyed hearing her name on his lips.

"You have the Duke's permission to address him as 'Bicky'. That will simplify matters." Being on such an uneven social scale, it would have been an unforgivable breech of protocol, but Bicky had always been a good sport.

Caro raised both eyebrows. "On intimate terms with His Grace… the Duke of Hetherington?"

"Yes, Caro." Evie pointed to the ceiling. "See, it hasn't collapsed on us and I'm sure the earth is still spinning." Turning back to Tom, she continued, "There are several house guests attending tonight's dinner."

He nodded. "Bicky already ran through them with me."

Of course, he had. How remiss of her, Evie thought, her mental tone mocking. "So, if I say Charlotte, you'll know I mean…"

"Lady Chambers, married to Lord Chambers. Matthew to his friends."

Evie prompted, "And you will address him as…"

"The first time, I will address him as Lord Chambers. From therein, it will be my lord or, if he gives me leave, Chambers."

By the end of the evening, Evie suspected Tom would be invited to refer to him as Matthew. No doubt about it.

Feeling an impish need to trip him up, Evie shot out, "Gloriana."

"You mean, Lady Gloriana, the Duke's... or rather, Bicky's cousin. She is married to the younger son of the Earl of Aspendale." Tom's eyes filled with mirth. "Do you think she will inherit the Dowager Duchess's pearls?"

Well, well. Bicky had been thorough.

"Yes, I can see you'll do very well. But if you happen to get tangled up, fall back on my lady or my lord."

Tom smiled. "Unless I happen to be talking with Mr. Mark Harper, heir to his cousin, the Earl of Chatterlain. In which case, I'll refer to him as Harper." He shrugged. "Or Mark."

Feeling almost superfluous, Evie clasped her hands and twiddled her thumbs. "Now, we must find you a suitable profession."

Tom nodded. "That has been taken care of."

"It has?"

He nodded again. "I did well enough in the oil fields to never have to work another day in my life."

Evie wavered for a moment. He had sounded so convincing, she had no trouble believing him. "Tell me more." She knew the others were bound to ask questions. After all, most of them... well, all of them had inherited their money. The concept of actually making it by striking it lucky would be beyond their comprehension.

Evie tapped her chin and revised her opinion as she remembered there had been some lucky titled landowners who'd struck it lucky with coal...

Slipping a hand into his pocket he said, "Back in 1914, I started out as a wildcatter in Tulsa, Oklahoma. Soon after, I purchased my first drilling rights." He gave her a winning smile. "The rest is far too... oily to go into. Needless to say, I struck oil."

"Indeed."

"I should add, your brother has been instrumental in assisting me with my investments."

"He has?" For a moment, Evie forgot they were creating a credible story to tell the others. Frowning, she ran through every possible situation he might encounter in the drawing room. "Oh, remind me again why you're on such familiar terms with Bicky."

"The war. We met briefly at the Battle of the Somme. The arduous experience has created many long-lasting friendships."

"Yet, he never mentioned you," Evie said testily.

"I think you'll be hard pressed to find anyone who willingly brings up the subject of the war and, if they do, the references will be very vague. We all prefer to put those dark years behind us."

Evie felt a shiver run up and down her spine.

To her surprise, he added, "After serving under British command, I then joined the American Expeditionary Forces staying with them until the end of the war."

"Fine. Now... Table manners."

He grinned. "Luckily, I have been feeding myself for as long as I can remember." She must have looked uncertain because Tom went on to add, "I promise I will keep my elbows off the table and refrain from talking with my mouth full."

"I didn't mean to imply you have sloppy manners. Only that... There is a delicate balance. Conversation is kept light, casual... amiable but lively. Of course, I'm sure you can manage all that." Feeling slightly on edge, Evie persevered. "After dinner, the ladies will withdraw to the drawing room, leaving the gentleman to smoke their cigars and drink their port. I've never been privy to the conversations that go on, so I'm afraid you'll be on your own."

"I believe I will be capable of holding my end of it without embarrassing you... Evie."

"What if someone brings up the subject of investments?"

"I would most likely mention your brother's exemplary handling of my investments. Let's assume it won't come up since the English don't really care to talk about money. But I will be prepared without going overboard with details or aspiring to pretentions I don't possess. While independently wealthy, I'm still at heart a wildcatter." He shrugged. "Still slightly rough around the edges and quite proud of it. It will fit with their idea of a self-made American millionaire."

Caro leaned in and asked in a soft murmur, "What exactly is a wildcatter?"

"A prospector," Evie murmured back. "They usually sink oil wells but they also participate in risky business ventures." Which would fit in nicely with her earlier remarks to Bicky regarding wealthy Americans and their willingness to take risks.

"What if someone suggests dancing?" Caro asked.

Tom gave them both a brisk smile.

Evie suspected he would have no trouble whisking her around a ballroom. "I doubt that will happen. Eventually, I believe we will tackle the subject of today's shooting. That should take care of conversation for the rest of the evening. We will all be much too preoccupied with suppositions to even consider the idea of dancing." Evie stopped. She only ever prattled on when she felt flustered. And she definitely felt out of sorts. Not in a dispirited way but rather...

Evie fiddled with her bracelet. Pressing her fingers against her wrist, she felt her pulse racing. "Right... Well. I believe we now have everything sorted out."

"Not quite," Tom said.

"Oh? What else is there to discuss?"

"I actually feel I should warn you," he said.

Pressing her hand to her heart, Evie asked, "Warn me? About what?"

"My intention to discreetly question the guests."

Evie yelped, "Whatever for?"

"I assume they all knew you were coming here."

She gave a reluctant nod.

"I'd like to know if they mentioned it to anyone else." Before she could object, he added, "Someone took a shot at you, not once but twice. That took some premeditation." He took a step toward her. "Someone planned it with meticulous precision."

Unable to contain her shock, she burst out, "Are you suggesting the Duke of Hetherington's guests are being held under suspicion?"

CHAPTER 9

Pre-dinner jitters...

*E*vie's mind swirled with too much new information to the point where she couldn't tell the difference between fact or fiction. Her otherwise monosyllabic chauffeur had strung so many sentences together, she had come close to swaying on the spot.

Had he entertained as many thoughts while driving her around? And... and what would happen after all this business was sorted out? How could she ever reinstate the status quo between them? Never mind that she'd been trying to lower the barriers...

In less than an hour, Mr. Tom Winchester had

demolished every intangible barrier that had stood between them.

"Do you think anyone in the household staff will recognize you as my chauffeur?" Evie asked as they strode down the stairs.

Tom gave her a lifted eyebrow look. "You tell me, Evie."

Evie almost missed the next step. As much as she'd wanted Tom to abandon all formalities and address her by her first name, Evie thought she would need more time to get used to it. Not because it created social awkwardness between them but because…

Well, because she rather liked the way her name sounded on his lips and she knew she shouldn't because…

Never mind why, Evie told herself and said, "We knew each other when we were young. Then, you moved away and we lost touch. That should take care of reducing the amount of detailed information we need to know about each other."

Reaching the bottom of the stairs, Evie placed her hand on his arm. "I think I need another minute."

The sound of lively chatter wafted toward them. A footman strode by carrying a tray of glasses. Another footman followed with another tray. Over the next few minutes, they watched a parade of household staff heading toward the dining room, carrying decanted wines and savory dishes which would most likely be served cold. Evie expected Larkin to appear at any minute and head toward the dining room to cast his eagle-eyed inspection over the table setting.

A wave of laughter reached them with Bicky's voice booming over it.

"He certainly knows how to entertain," Tom observed.

"Yes, Bicky's house parties are famous. Over the years, I've attended many hosted by more people than I thought I knew and his continue to stand out as the most memorable ones."

"I suppose this one is no exception," Tom said.

"No, in fact, this one beats them all, but for very different and obvious reasons." Evie released a shuddering breath. "I hope the authorities can get to the bottom of this."

"If not them, then us."

Evie's eyebrows rose. "You actually believe you can make some sort of progress and discover the culprit?"

He gave a small shrug. "There's no harm in trying. Being on the inside might give us an advantage. The different perspective could provide us with a clue that might not otherwise be available to the police."

Evie wondered if anyone in the village had noticed anything unusual or heard something... A passing remark, anything that might suggest someone meant to do her harm.

"Do you remember the first swimming lesson I gave you?" Tom asked, his tone matter of fact.

It took a moment for Evie to realize he expected her to make something up on the spot. "Y-yes, I'm sure I do. Let me think. We were at the end of the jetty. I remember we'd been picnicking by the lake and it had been an unbearably hot day. You told me to go back to the shore and wade in but I refused. I always got into trouble for defying orders. I wanted to join in the fun so I watched the others jump off the jetty and in a moment of foolish valor, I jumped in. I sunk to the bottom and when I resurfaced, you were right there by my side calling me a puppy dog and telling me to kick my legs and move my arms. Before I knew it, we had reached the shoreline, safe and sound."

He watched her in silence, finally he asked, "Did that really happen?"

Evie beamed up at him. "Actually, I had a personal swimming instructor." But she suddenly liked her made-up story better. Tilting her head in thought, she added, "If we're asked the same question at different times and we each give a different response, I can always accuse you of seeing things through rose tinted glasses or remembering events in a way that makes you look fabulous."

He chuckled. "There's nothing wrong with that."

Scooping in a breath, she nodded. "Let's go in, shall we?"

To her surprise, he gave her his arm.

It seemed natural to slip her hand through it and rest it on his forearm. Crazy, but wonderful. "By the way, I believe the Red Sox are up against the Yankees on May 1."

"Did you read that in the society pages?" he asked under his breath.

"I don't recall... How do you think they'll go?"

He barely moved his lips when he said in a tight voice, "I'm sure they'll do just fine."

Evie and Tom strode into the drawing room in time to hear the tail end of Bicky's conversation.

"...When Evie mentioned Tom had landed in London, I urged her to get in touch with him and invite him up to Yarborough straightaway."

Evie leaned in and whispered, "I think His Grace has been warming up our audience."

At a glance, there didn't appear to be anything wrong with the Duke. On close inspection, Evie noticed a slight bulge on his arm where the bandage had been applied. Also, his arm hung limply by his side.

Seeing them, Bicky exclaimed, "I've been telling them all about you, Tom. Come on in and meet everyone. Everyone, this is Tom Winchester."

Evie realized they'd left out a pertinent detail.

Tom Winchester of the Massachusetts Winchesters?

Tom Winchester of the Oklahoma oil field Winchesters?

Bicky played host and made proper introductions. Rather than stopping for lengthy chats, he kept Tom moving along.

She heard Tom say to Mark Harper his arrival could not have been better timed as he'd always promised Evie's grandmother he'd keep her safe.

"And are you here on business or for pleasure, Mr. Winchester?" Charlotte asked.

"Tom, please. Evie has nothing but high praise for her adopted country so I thought I'd finally come and see it for myself."

It took Tom less than half an hour to be on first name terms with everyone, a feat he managed to accomplish with admirable ease.

At the first opportunity, Evie slipped out and headed for the dining room to check on the place settings for the night. Wanting to do what she could, she had no intention of letting Tom out of her sight for longer than a few minutes... Just in case someone cornered him with a difficult question.

As expected, she found his name across the table from her so she did the unthinkable and swapped place cards.

When she returned to the drawing room, she made a beeline for Bicky.

"I think this is going rather well," Bicky murmured.

"I agree. It's almost as if he'd been born to play the

role," Evie mused and wondered how much more there could be to Tom Winchester.

When Larkin announced dinner, they all moved toward the dining room chatting with ease and a spark of enthusiasm over the newcomer.

As they took their places, Tom leaned in and grumbled, "Did you have anything to do with the seating arrangements?"

"What do you mean?" Evie whispered back.

"It is unusual to be seated next to one's partner," he said.

Partner? "Fine. I might have fiddled around with the name place cards. Admit it, you would not have been pleased to have been seated next to Lady Charlotte. She does tend to go on…"

"Was I seated next to her?" Tom asked.

"Does it matter?"

"It does matter since the aim is for me to make discreet inquiries."

Larkin approached with a platter, lowering it so Tom could help himself. Evie held her breath and wondered if Tom would know he needed to only help himself to an adequate portion and not shovel all the food in. Sighing, Evie suddenly felt like a complete and utter snob. She had no doubt Tom had already observed the butler making the rounds of the table.

"Tom. What are your thoughts on this business of prohibition?" Lord Chambers asked.

Evie nearly dropped her fork.

"Generally, I think making too many rules only taunts people into finding ways to break them," Tom said. "From what I understand, there is some concern about the possible rise in crime."

"And do you feel personally affected by it all?" Charlotte asked and took a long sip of her wine.

"Where's your interest coming from, Charlotte?" Evie interjected. "Are you afraid you'll have to learn to live without your brandy fruitcake?"

"If forced to abstain," Lady Charlotte responded, "I do think I would find a way to rebel. It's not as if I have brandy fruitcake morning, noon and night but I couldn't possibly go without."

"Larkin," Bicky called out. "What's for dessert?"

"Jellied Port and Brandied Peaches, Your Grace."

"And for the main?"

"Medallion of spring lamb with a white wine sauce, Your Grace."

"I see. I'm afraid I will have to take a stand here. Being the Lord and master of this household, I hereby declare there will be no more talk of prohibition here. We depend on our occasional drop far too much to risk tempting the fates."

Exchanging a look of amusement with Tom, Evie then leaned in and whispered, "Charlotte enjoys wringing everything she can out of a subject. We all suspect it's because she has a morbid fear of silence. If

Bicky hadn't put an end to it, we'd be talking about prohibition until the sun comes up."

Bicky drew everyone's attention again by saying, "By the way, the Sergeant will be dropping by tomorrow to ask us all a few questions. He thought the ladies might need today to get over the shock of the ghastly experience."

Charlotte laughed. "Suddenly, I feel as though we should get our stories straight. I've never been questioned by the police before."

Everyone at the table concurred, expressing their lack of experience with the authorities. Now, they were more intrigued than worried.

"Did the police inspect the grounds?" Tom asked.

"They certainly did," Bicky replied. "If they found anything, they didn't tell me. Personally, I doubt it. According to Larkin, the grass is too lush and there are no signs of it being trampled."

Tom took a leisurely sip of his wine before saying, "With your permission, I would like to have a word with your estate agent and stable manager tomorrow."

"Feel free," Bicky said. "Although, I hope you don't mean to imply one of them did it."

"Not at all," Tom assured him. "But they might have noticed something."

"What makes you think they'll speak with you, Tom?" Charlotte asked. "They might not feel inclined to open up to a complete stranger."

Evie's light laughter tinkled across the table. "Tom has a way about him. He gets on well with everyone and makes himself comfortable in any situation. He can easily lower the social barriers. He's quite down to earth. In fact, he didn't wish to impose on Bicky and had suggested staying at the pub."

"Matthew and I stayed at a pub once," Charlotte mused. "I had been reading a romance and noticed our ancestors used to break their long trips in pubs so I thought it would be fun to try it out."

"Where did you stay?" Evie asked.

Charlotte smiled enthusiastically, "*Ye Olde Trip to Jerusalem.* The cellars are carved from the rocks beneath Nottingham Castle. The establishment can be traced all the way back to the 1180s and had been used as a stopover point for crusaders on their way to meet with Richard the Lionheart. Matthew believes one of his ancestors stayed there so we spent our stay looking for carvings or some sort of scratching on a wall."

"You think he might have scribbled his name?" Evie asked.

"It's not as crazy as it sounds," Charlotte said. "His initials are carved on several doors at home."

Home being his Lordship's country pile dating back to the Norman conquest, Evie thought.

Charlotte seemed to be on a roll. "Tom, what do you make of English hospitality?"

To his credit, Tom took his time responding. He

also made a point of looking at Evie as if to reassure her he had everything under control. "Beyond compare, Lady Charlotte."

"Oh, please do call me Charlotte," she laughed. "Anyhow, you say that because no one took a shot at you."

"I'm prepared to give everyone the benefit of the doubt. I'm sure the Duke did not mean to organize a shooter to liven up the event."

Charlotte's eyes brightened. "I feel a however coming on."

Tom nodded. "However, since you mentioned it, someone has taken a shot at someone in the house. Regardless, I wouldn't allow that to influence my opinion of the Duke's hospitality."

"But you take the attempt on someone's life as a personal affront?" Charlotte asked.

Everyone who'd been holding murmured conversations stopped to listen to Tom's response.

With a smile in place, he sent his gaze skating around the table. "I wouldn't go so far as to say that, but I am interested to find out if Evie has any enemies."

Charlotte sounded shocked when she asked, "You think the shot fired had been intended for her?"

"We can't know for sure," Evie said.

"I'm interested to know what Tom will do with the guilty party... if they are ever found." Charlotte's voice now carried a degree of intrigue and exhilaration, possibly over the prospect of Tom Winchester wielding his revolver and taking matters into his own hands.

"I will make sure justice is served," he said.

"That's a rather enigmatic answer."

"You'll have to excuse my wife," Matthew piped in. "I believe she has been reading too many stories about the Wild West and thinks you might gather together a posse and chase down the culprit." He turned to his wife. "No one will be strung up."

"No, but they might be drawn and quartered." Charlotte smiled. "Tom, in case you are not acquainted with our history, we were once very fond of the hung, drawn and quartered punishment." Taking a sip of her wine, she set her glass down and asked. "Isn't that the name of a pub? It rings a bell."

Mark Harper nodded. "Yes, I believe it's near the Tower of London. It's relatively new. They have an excellent menu."

Charlotte remarked, "I take it you have dined there."

"I have," Mark agreed.

"I'm curious. What were you doing near the Tower of London?" Charlotte asked. "That's rather a long distance from your town house."

Evie recalled Caro saying Mark had been intent on sowing his wild oats so she imagined he had been there to meet a paramour.

Mark hid his smile. "What anyone else does. Sightseeing, of course."

Evie leaned in and whispered, "While Charlotte enjoys wringing as much as she can out of a subject, she also excels at digressing. Mark my word, she will somehow bring the conversation back to prohibition."

Right on cue, Charlotte said, "I've been thinking... The majority of liturgical churches require sacramental wine for their service. Tom, has prohibition reached the church steps?"

"What did I tell you," Evie murmured.

CHAPTER 10

Men have sewing circles too...

$\mathcal{E}$vie glanced over at the door, her nerves on edge. The ladies had withdrawn over half an hour ago leaving the gentlemen to their port and cigars and male related subjects.

She imagined them all huddled around the dinner table grumbling and beating their club sticks while muttering pompous exclamations about their lot in life.

Glancing around the drawing room, she met Penelope's gaze. When they shared a small smile, Evie considered joining her for a chat. Then she remembered Penelope had never been big on chatting. Not unless she had something to complain about; her maid being too slow-witted, her cook being too predictable, her butler flirting with the maids...

Regardless, she decided to make an effort. Evie shifted but before she could get up, Bicky's sister, Lady Elizabeth, settled beside Evie.

Elizabeth lifted her glass of cognac in a salute. Clearly, she had needed something strong to get her through the shock of nearly losing her brother.

"You are far braver than I would be in your place," Elizabeth said.

Evie smiled. "Whatever do you mean?"

Elizabeth leaned in. "Before dinner, I called in on Bicky to see how he was getting on and he confided in me."

This did not bode well. If the circle of secrecy continued to expand, then everyone would know about Tom...

Evie didn't need to prompt Elizabeth for more details.

"He said someone tried to run you off the road. That leads me to believe you are, in fact, the target." Elizabeth lowered her voice. "That bullet had your name written on it."

Relieved to hear they could continue with their charade without having to offer further explanations, Evie said, "Really Elizabeth, we can't jump to conclusions."

"How can you be so untroubled by it? In your place,

I'd be hiding under the bed. Actually, I'd be on my way to the nearest port, hoping to jump on the first ship I could find to take me back home. First the rumors about you sniffing around for husband number two and now this."

Had someone tried to scare her off? Evie lifted her chin in defiance. "I try to ignore the rumors and assume they are started by people who do not know me."

Elizabeth held her gaze. "Like it or not, your presence here will make many people unhappy."

Elizabeth had never spoken of it before. So, Evie felt compelled to ask, "What have you heard?"

"Nothing new. In fact, it's been the same morose complaints about you having all the advantages of wealth and position and taking away any worthwhile opportunity from more deserving well-bred girls."

Evie pursed her lips. "I should take offense, but I won't. Perhaps I should inscribe a message on my forehead stating I have no intention of ever marrying again."

"Would it fit? You do have a wide forehead but I fear it wouldn't be wide enough." Elizabeth shook her head. "No, you'll need something more succinct than that. Let me think. Is there a single word that would denote your intention, clearly stating you are no longer interested in marriage?" Elizabeth stared at her for a moment. "I do not believe such a word exists. Therefore, it is an impossibility. No one will ever believe you have withdrawn from the idea of marriage. It's almost unnatural. And if you say time will only tell, I will have to contradict you because time may not be on your side."

Evie chortled. "Elizabeth, I never knew you could be so dramatic and such a pessimist and…" Evie drew in a long breath. "Surely, the person behind all this won't push it that far? It all seems so petty."

"Look around you, Evie. We are in the gold drawing room, not the blue drawing room. That's the one with a bullet hole in one of its windows."

Evie looked toward the door again and wished the gentlemen would hurry up and guzzle their port. She needed to speak with Tom. The sooner they could put their heads together and identify the real target, the better.

Evie returned her attention to Elizabeth who laughed and said, "Oh, please. Don't give me that pitying look. I'm not being ridiculous."

Evie smiled. "Not ridiculous, but perhaps you are overreacting, just a teeny-weeny bit. Think about it. There is only one person who has shown great interest in my return. Can you really picture Lady Wainscot wielding a rifle?"

Elizabeth tilted her head in thought. "She is desperate to see her daughters wedded, preferably to titled gentlemen."

The door to the drawing room opened and the exclusively male sewing circle strode in. Evie studied their expressions for signs they might have been struck by some sort of epiphany, revealing a fully formed explanation for the day's events.

Seeing Tom heading toward the window, Evie rolled her eyes. She supposed if the weather had not been so mild, the fireplace might have been lit, providing an equally if not more engaging spot in which to gather one's thoughts.

"Did you find the after-dinner conversation illuminating?" she asked Tom.

He gave a pensive nod.

"Do share."

"We talked at great length about motor car cooling systems."

Evie didn't bother hiding her disappointment. "I thought you wanted to make discreet inquiries."

"In my own roundabout way, I did. Bicky remains the only one who knew you were arriving early and he didn't mention it to anyone in his household."

"Before you ask, I am absolutely certain Bicky didn't try to kill me. Nor did he stage a scenario where he might have been wounded."

"I didn't mean to imply... Anyhow, there is something I didn't tell you. It has to do with the incident out on the road." He slipped his hand inside his pocket and drew a small object out.

Evie looked down at his hand. "What is it?"

"It's a bullet. Or, at least, what's left of it."

"Oh."

"I'm not sure if you noticed a sudden jolt during our drive."

"Yes, I did. Right after I saw the birds taking flight."

"I lost temporary control of the motor. Anyhow, after our arrival, I drove out there again and found this bullet on the road."

Proof they'd been shot at…

"At first, I thought it might have penetrated the grille and caused some damage to the cooling pump. When I returned and had to wait for Caro to deliver your message, I had a look under the motor…"

Evie tried to keep up with his otherwise precise description of what he'd found, but she couldn't get past the idea of someone actually trying to shoot her twice.

"Out on the road," he continued, "I caught a glint of light. It appeared to come from a high place, perhaps a tree. But, even with the best gun, the trajectory of this bullet could not have been possible from high up on a tree."

Evie bit the edge of her lip. "You're saying there were two people."

"Yes. One up on a tree keeping a lookout and another on the ground with a rifle."

Her eyebrows drew downward. "You think that's

because otherwise the bullet would not have penetrated between the gaps…"

He nodded. "Remember, we were taking a slight curve, so the wheel turned enough to expose a gap."

Her lips parted. "He must be an excellent shot."

He agreed. "Probably military trained."

Evie shook her head. "Not necessarily. In fact, you'll find many excellent shots in the area." Heavens, if it came down to expertise with a rifle, there would be an abundance of suspects.

CHAPTER 11

Gossip, musings and revelations

The next morning, Caro strode into Evie's room carrying a tray. Evie scrambled to sit up. When Caro set the tray down, she turned her attention to drawing the curtains open.

"I'm almost tempted to stop you, Caro." Evie had slept poorly, tossing and turning as the images of the day before swirled around her mind.

Closing her eyes, she took a long sip of tea. "How is everyone this morning?"

"Busy as always and somehow still managing to chat about yesterday. I haven't heard anything new." Caro brought out a couple of blouses and selected one.

"By the way, the delivery boy brought a package for you yesterday."

"Oh, wonderful. My soap. To think, I should have headed into the village today for my beauty treatment but I gave away my time slot to Miss Wainscot. I hope she appreciates it."

"If you don't mind me asking, why did you do that, milady?"

Evie tipped her head back. "Oh, I suppose we were trying to sweeten Miss Wainscot up so she wouldn't delve too deeply. In the end, I think she ended up finding out more than we wanted."

Belatedly, Evie wondered if that might actually be a good thing. If Miss Wainscot decided to put two and two together, she might have told her mama there had been a Mr. Winchester asking to see Evie and, in her opinion, the two were sweet on each other. That would certainly divert Lady Wainscot's attention. Perhaps even pacify her. If Evie had her sights on an untitled gentleman then her attention wouldn't stray to a titled bachelor. Then again, Lady Wainscot might decide Mr. Winchester could be a good catch for one of her daughters…

"Well, at least you're smiling now, milady. Things can't be so bad, after all." Caro held up an ensemble for Evie's approval. The silk blouse with tiny white daisies had a scooped collar and short sleeves. Perfect for a pleasant spring day. Caro then brought out a selection of hats and settled on a straw one with a dainty black cat curled up beside the light green band.

"How did Tom do last night?" Caro asked. "Was his performance to your satisfaction?"

Evie's eyes brightened. "He carried himself extremely well. At no point did I think of him as my chauffeur."

Caro stared at her, her eyes not blinking.

Evie shrugged. "Who would have thought? Tom turned out to be quite a conversationalist. He never once stumbled."

"So, no one suspected."

"No, at least, I don't think they did."

"And did you find out anything worthwhile?"

"Perhaps." Evie drank her tea. She always preferred to have a beverage in bed and then join the rest downstairs for a proper breakfast. When she attended house parties, she always found this to be the best way to set the pace for the day.

"Caro."

"Yes, milady."

"I hate to ask this, but I feel I must." Evie counted to three and drew in a fortifying breath. "Did you happen to mention my early arrival to anyone?"

"Of course not, milady. As far as anyone knew, you were arriving today."

Shame on her for feeling the need to ask, Evie thought. Of course, she could always trust Caro. "Poor

Mrs. Saunders," Evie remarked. "I know she runs the household like a well-oiled machine, but it can't be easy to have people arriving early without first letting her know. Had she been informed about the early arrival of the others?"

"She knew, milady. Cook didn't seem to mind. It only meant preparing an extra meal and she loves the challenge."

Evie cringed. "Now I feel awkward for not having informed anyone." In reality, she felt relieved because it meant none of the household staff had known she would be here a day ahead of schedule. It would only take a slip of the tongue to alert the entire village of something unexpected happening at the big house.

"The bath should be ready in a moment, milady." Caro disappeared into the adjoining room.

Evie finished her tea and as she put her cup down, a thought settled in her mind.

If no one had known about her change of plans, then how had the shooter known to wait for her along the road?

Evie rushed through her bath and hurried downstairs only to find the other guests had slept in.

"Bicky. Has Tom come down?"

"About half an hour ago," Bicky said. "He had a

nibble of something or other and then he said he wanted to have a wander around the estate." Bicky set his cup down. "I say, he was very good last night. I hope you bring him back for another stay."

Glancing over at Larkin who stood at attention several steps behind Bicky, Evie leaned in and whispered, "You seem to forget he is my chauffeur."

"Oh... Yes... Of course. Well, there you go. I still wouldn't mind having him stay. Isn't that odd? I think the war changed us all. As mama says, war tends to bring down barriers."

"Not to that extent, I'm sure."

Bicky shrugged. "You never know. Last night, he told us a cracking good tale about his days in the oil fields in Oklahoma. Very amusing. I think he would be a great addition..."

"Is that what you talked about while you were puffing on your cigars?"

"That and other things."

"Did the others prod him for information?" Evie asked.

Bicky shook his head. "I think you'll find men are a different breed. Not as inquisitive as the ladies appear to be." He held his cup up and gestured to Larkin who promptly filled it with coffee.

"Would you care for some more coffee, my lady?" Larkin offered.

"Thank you, Larkin." Feeling revitalized, she got up

and helped herself to some bacon and eggs. "So, what time do you expect Clara to arrive today?"

"Afternoon." Bicky set his knife and fork down. "She said she had a few more errands to run. Although, what they might be I have no idea."

The others began to trickle in, each one expressing their delight over a night well spent.

"It's just occurred to me," Charlotte exclaimed as she sat next to Evie. "We're in the midst of a mystery." Glancing over at Larkin, she lowered her tone. "I wonder if the butler did it…"

CHAPTER 12

It's a matter of loyalty

Evie strolled toward the folly and found Tom by a large elm tree. "There you are."

"Good morning... Evie."

Tom wore a different suit to the one he'd worn the day before and still looked magnificent in it. "Have you made any new discoveries?"

He shook his head. "I've had a close inspection of the surrounding trees. None of the branches appear to have been disturbed." He turned and looked toward the house. "The gunman might have been in plain sight. It's amazing that in a house such as this one no one noticed him."

"That's because everyone is busy with their duties," Evie observed. "You'd be hard pressed to find any of the servants lingering with nothing to do."

"They do take breaks," Tom remarked. "Unfortunately, the yard is on the other side of the house."

As Tom gazed into the distance, Evie said, "This should cheer you up. I had a fruitful morning. The information should have come to me before, but I'm guessing it must have been waiting for the dust to settle and my mind to clear enough for me to perceive the fact."

"Which is?" Tom prompted.

"No one knew of my early arrival. I've been thinking it all along, but not really paying too much attention. How does one go about planning to shoot someone if they don't know when their intended target will be arriving?"

Tom held her gaze for a moment and finally said, "They wait."

Oh, that hadn't occurred to her. Now she would have to start from scratch again and try to find out how the news about her journey to Yarborough had spread. Evie wondered if she needed to turn her focus to her own household.

Caro and Tom were in the clear, but what of the others? She knew news could be transmitted from upstairs to the downstairs staff quicker than on a telegraph wire.

"Have you spoken with the estate workers?" she asked.

"I was just on my way over to the stables."

"Would you mind if I accompany you?"

He drew in a breath. "If you wish."

There had been a hint of hesitation, so she felt the need to ask, "I get the feeling you think my presence will hinder your investigation."

He gave her a brisk smile. "Not at all. In fact, I think most of the estate workers will welcome the chance to see the Countess of Woodridge up close."

Evie grinned. "I think you meant to say, the notorious Evangeline Parker."

They found the path leading to the stables and strolled side by side.

Smiling at her, Tom asked, "How did you earn your notoriety?"

Evie laughed. "Without even trying. I simply married one of their own. Apparently, that cast a shadow of doubt over me because, surely, I must have employed some sort of cunningness to land him."

"Did you?"

Evie should have taken offense. After all, debutantes were encouraged to attract the attention of the most desirable and eligible partners by whatever means possible. "During my first and, as it turned out, my only season in London, I failed to show any interest in the gentlemen introduced to me. Then, I attended my first house party at Bicky's. The rest, as they say, is history. I simply fell in love."

"So, it was a love match," he mused.

"Yes, as unusual as it sounds, we did fall in love and we stayed in love. Before you ask, I should tell you I have no intention of marrying again. Rumor has it, I pose a threat to the latest batch of debutantes." She tilted her head in thought. "I wish they would stop using me as an excuse..."

Tom laughed. "You make them sound like biscuits just out of the oven."

Light and fluffy, Evie mused. "They are well-trained and taught to meet everyone's expectations. It's rare to find one with individual character traits. I suspect it's all beaten out of them. I don't really mean to criticize but I seem to be paying a high prize for being myself."

They reached the stables and were greeted by Mr. Beecham, the agent, who informed them he'd already had a word with the estate workers.

"Are you able to account for everyone's whereabouts yesterday?" Tom asked. "They might need to provide proof to the Sergeant."

Mr. Beecham bobbed his head in thought. "Everyone has their tasks to perform throughout the day. If the job is not done, then someone is bound to notice. His Grace employs hard, dedicated workers and, needless to say, they are all loyal to him."

Evie's brows narrowed slightly. "How do they feel about the Duchess?"

Mr. Beecham took a deep swallow. "I know these men. They are here to work and not to meddle in other people's affairs."

Strange choice of words, Evie thought.

Mr. Beecham looked away and then down at the ground. Thinking she'd made him uncomfortable, Evie turned to gaze around her. Noticing a stable boy grooming a horse, she excused herself and strode away. As she approached, the young boy tipped his hat and promptly continued with his task.

"She is a beauty," Evie remarked.

"His Grace keeps a fine stable, milady."

"Do you enjoy working here?" she asked.

The young lad's cheeks turned bright red. "I do, milady. Very much."

"Does the Duchess ride?"

The boy bent down to run the brush along the horse's leg and mumbled, "Not any more, milady."

"Oh, did something happen?"

"She came off… at the last hunt."

"I see. I suppose she doesn't care much for getting back on a horse."

"Not likely, milady. She then took her whip to the horse…" The boy broke off almost as if he felt he'd said too much.

Bending down slightly, Evie said, "How dreadful. I'm sure His Grace can't have been pleased about that."

"No, indeed, milady." The boy looked about and lowered his voice. "He banned her... I mean, Her Grace, from the stables. Said if he ever caught her here, he would take a whip to her and see how she liked it."

Well said, Bicky.

Evie couldn't help shuddering. Cruelty to people who could defend themselves could be forgiven, to a point, but cruelty to defenseless animals was beyond the pale.

As she stroked the horse, she looked over at Tom and Mr. Beecham. The steward's remark about loyalty had struck her as odd. She tried to remember his exact words.

They are loyal to him.

Not to the family, Evie thought, but rather, to him.

If any of the estate workers disliked the Duchess, they might express their opinions within their peer group, but certainly not in the presence of the family. And now... such an attitude would make perfect sense.

Had she read too much into the agent's remark?

The estate workers would have heard about the Duchess using her whip on a horse. That would be enough to withdraw their loyalty.

That made Evie wonder if they had any thoughts about her. And, if they did, would they act on it? She'd never dream of harming an animal, but she remained an outsider. With some people holding a low opinion of her, locals working at the estate might take it upon themselves to choose sides.

Smiling at the boy, she turned to leave only to stop. What did it matter if the estate workers didn't care for Clara? She hadn't been targeted. In fact, she remained safe and sound and probably having the time of her life in London…

"The point is…" Evie murmured. "Clara committed a hideous crime. Yet the estate workers haven't taken action against her."

Not a single one of them would have reason to target Bicky or Evie.

CHAPTER 13

"So you think I'm the murderer? What do I have to do to convince you that I'm not, be the next victim?" — *from 'Charade' 1963*

When Tom finished talking with Mr. Beecham, he expressed a desire to spread further afield and visit some of the cottages near the large house, but Evie prompted him with a reminder they were attending a house party.

"Everyone usually meets in the library at this time for refreshments."

"Usually but not always?" Tom asked. Clearly trying to excuse himself from the activity.

"We should stick close to the house," Evie said. "Remember, the Sergeant will be dropping by today."

When they strode into the library, they found everyone engaged in lively conversation. Without exception, they all turned and included Tom in their greeting.

"You seem to have become a party favorite," Evie whispered.

"Only until the novelty wears off," he whispered back.

They both approached a table and helped themselves to coffee.

"I take it there's a lot of tea drinking and food consumed at these type of house parties," Tom said.

Evie nodded. "We need our energy for everything else in-between. There's nothing more amiable than to share a bit of news between sips of tea or coffee. Come to think of it, I find drinking tea or coffee far more conducive to lowering people's guards than a glass of wine."

Tom gave her a brisk smile. "I'll try to keep that in mind. Although, I'm not sure I'd be comfortable spilling all my secrets over a cup of tea."

She looked at him without saying anything. It took her a moment to realize she had been held mesmerized by the simple conversation. Or, rather, by the fact he could hold a conversation without any sense of awkwardness interfering. It almost felt as if they'd known each other all their lives.

Moments later, a footman strode in and relayed a message to the butler.

Clearing his throat, Larkin announced, "The Dowager Duchess."

Bicky's mama, the Dowager Duchess, entered and gazed around the library. When she found the object of her vexation, she stopped and, wrapping her fingers around the handle of the umbrella she carried around everywhere, she said, "Bicky. There you are. I see you are alive and well now but why is it that I had to wait to be informed of your injury until this morning. There I was, enjoying my morning tea when my butler, yes indeed, my butler expressed his well wishes for your speedy recovery. He knew of the attempt on your life well before I did."

"Good morning, mama. As you can see, I'm quite all right."

"All right? All right? Stand there with your arm hanging by your side long enough and you will have pigeons nesting on your head."

"Mama. I am perfectly fine. Dr. Higgins merely recommended resting and so I am resting my arm by not overexerting it with unnecessary movements."

"Be that as it may, why was I not informed? The news spread right throughout the village and possibly beyond the county before it reached my ears. How do you think I felt when villagers stopped me to offer their well wishes?"

Bicky bowed his head. "Please accept my deepest apologies, mama. We did not wish to burden you with unnecessary worry."

The Dowager Duchess gave an unladylike snort. "You seem to be downplaying the severity of your near miss. If you'd died, Alexander Fleshling, your cousin thrice removed, would have acquired your title. Do you think I would have looked forward to spending the rest of my life with a complete stranger taking your place?"

"Mama, you know as well as I do, there are risks involved in everything we undertake in life. I hope you will be able to put it all behind you. Have some fruitcake. I have recently been made aware of how fortunate we should consider ourselves for having brandy in our cake."

The Dowager Duchess looked taken aback. "You want me to sit and enjoy a piece of cake when there is so much more I wish to say?"

Bicky took a step back. "More?"

"Much more." The Dowager gave a stiff nod. "As I made my way to visit poor Lady Wainscot who has been taken ill…"

Evie exchanged a look of surprise with the others.

The Dowager rested her other hand on the umbrella handle. "I received more second-hand news. On top of everything else, someone took it upon themselves to inform me the Countess of Woodridge has descended upon us."

"Mama."

"Yes, indeed. The Countess of Woodridge has arrived and news about her visit is sweeping throughout the county."

Tom leaned in and whispered, "Is it just me, or did she mean to imply you are some sort of plague sweeping through the countryside?"

Evie grinned. "No, she wouldn't be so crass. She only means to compare me to a storm, perhaps even a hurricane."

The Dowager's gaze shifted from her son, moving until she had located Tempest Woodridge as she had, no doubt, mentally referred to her.

"Ah, there you are, my dear." The Dowager's eyes sparkled as she gave Evie a small smile.

Evie smiled back. "Duchess, how good to see you again."

"To think you should have been addressing me as mama. But, oh no, despite the promise of a duchess's coronet, my Bicky was not good enough for you."

Evie approached her and, leaning in, greeted her properly. If anything, the Dowager never wavered from her intention to confuse people with her ever-changing opinions. It didn't bother Evie because she understood the Dowager employed the tactic to sit on the fence, reserving her true opinions to herself and the privileged few within her close circle.

"Well, then..." Bicky said. "Now that's all sorted out. Have some tea, mama."

"Tea? But I haven't finished yet." The Dowager gave a small nod. "Oh, yes. There is more. Even before I reached Lady Wainscot's house, I received a third piece of news." The Dowager turned and scrutinized everyone's reaction.

Evie resumed her place beside Tom, knowing full well the Dowager would now pin her attention on the newcomer because surely that had to be the third piece of news.

"Oh, yes. Here he is. I presume you are the very Mr. Winchester everyone is talking about."

Tom bowed his head slightly. "Your Grace."

"Oh, there's no brashness about him whatsoever. Well, well. At least, some of the rumors were incorrect." Turning to Evie, she said, "Nevertheless, everyone knows and once again, I am the last to be notified. Have you set a date?"

Teacups rattled on saucers.

Someone coughed. Evie thought she heard a snicker... or two.

"Well?" the Dowager demanded.

"I'm afraid you have been misinformed," Evie said.

The Dowager sputtered, "Misinformed? Are you suggesting I have been lied to? Who would dare play such a trick on me? Is he or is he not your current beau?"

Evie sighed and tried to decide if she should play the role or not. If she committed to the charade, she would have to see it through to some sort of completion. It would definitely give her a brief respite from overprotective mamas but what of the long term? Would she then fake a break-up? And what sort of impact would that have on her life?

Evie took a moment to mentally follow the trail of deceit until she saw herself having to explain the circumstances of her fabricated relationship and eventual break-up to her grandmother, not to mention, her mother.

"Duchess, Tom and I are very good childhood friends," Evie explained.

"And yet, I have never heard you mention him," the Dowager challenged.

Evie gave her an impish smile. "You must admit, from the moment we met, you felt overwhelmed by the presence of one American. How could I have introduced more to you? Surely you don't think me that wicked."

"True."

The Dowager appeared to take a moment to gather her thoughts. To Evie's surprise, she did not move to the window to do so.

"You must come for afternoon tea and tell me all about him," the Dowager invited.

"It would be my pleasure," Evie said.

"And bring Mr. Winchester with you." The Dowager tilted her head. "Winchester. Any relation to the Marquess of Winchester?"

Tom smiled. "No, Your Grace. I don't believe so."

"Is there any chance we might find a connection to him? Perhaps a distant one. The title is very old. In fact, it is the oldest English Marquessate still in existence. They keep finding heirs several times removed. You could be one of them."

Tom, bless his heart, indulged the Dowager with a simple, "Perhaps."

The Dowager brimmed. "Well, there you have it, Evangeline, you might end up becoming a Marchioness. That would be quite a coup for you."

Evie smiled. "Either that or we might have to engage the current Marquess in correspondence and offer our sincerest apologies for being presumptuous enough to suspect a connection."

Bicky made another attempt to distract his mama, stretching his hand toward a chair.

The Dowager lifted her chin. "Did I say I had finished speaking?"

In the ensuing silence, everyone took the opportunity to cross their legs, find a more comfortable spot or shift toward the edge of their seats. Whatever their response, they all knew they had front row seats to the Dowager's finest performance to date.

Bicky stepped back until he collided with a chair and sat down.

Tom took the opportunity to help himself to some fruitcake, remarking, "Quite good. I think I taste brandy." He took another bite and nodded. "Yes, the raisins must be soaked in it."

The Dowager scanned the room as if gathering everyone's attention to her. Clearing her throat, she lifted her chin and set a foot forward. Anyone watching her could have been forgiven if they thought she was about to burst into an operatic aria.

When someone coughed, the Dowager shot them a look that would have prompted anyone to offer an apology for the disruption.

"Now, where were we? Oh, yes. Burdened by all the news I had heard along the way and still rather shaken by my son's close encounter with the grim reaper, I finally arrived at Hainsley Hall, all along assuming I would be there to express my heartfelt wishes for a swift recovery from who knew what affliction when I discovered a grave piece of news to add to the multitude I had been collecting throughout the morning."

Everyone held their collective breaths.

"Lady Wainscot's houseguests were all in a state of mourning over the near fatal attempt on the young Miss Wainscot." Once again, the Dowager scanned the room, gaging everyone's response. Seeing everyone's wide-eyed expressions, she must have realized she was in the process of delivering fresh news, so she brightened. "Yes, you heard correctly. Someone tried to do away with Miss Wainscot." The Dowager's gaze landed on Evie. "And the finger of suspicion is being pointed directly at you, Evangeline Parker."

Oh, dear. This couldn't be good, Evie thought. The Dowager had just stripped her of her title. Belatedly, Evie pressed her hand to her chest and gaped. "Me?"

The Dowager gave a swift nod. "Yes, indeed. You."

Larkin cleared his throat and announced, "Sergeant Newbury."

The Dowager swung around to look at the newcomer. "Oh, I see. The authorities are taking prompt action and they've come to take Evangeline Parker away."

CHAPTER 14

The finger of suspicion

"I'm sure it's all a misunderstanding, Evie." Bicky stepped forward to stand between Evie and the Sergeant, his good hand placed in the small of his back.

Sergeant Newbury took out a notebook. "Begging your pardon, Your Grace. I am here to carry out the police inquiries we spoke of yesterday. If I could please see each and every one of you separately."

"Well, what do you propose we do?" the Dowager asked. "March out of the library to go stand out in the hall?"

Bicky said, "Larkin."

123

"Yes, Your Grace."

"Please show the Sergeant to the drawing room. That way, and if need be, we could all illustrate clearly where we were at the time of the shooting."

Larkin bowed his head slightly. "Very well, Your Grace." Turning to the Sergeant, he gestured to the door. "Please follow me."

After settling the Sergeant in the drawing room, Larkin returned. "The Sergeant wishes to speak with Viscount Maison."

Charles stood up and, straightening his jacket, said, "Wish me luck." He strode off, his manner somber yet full of valor.

A murmur made its way around the library.

"Good Lord," Tom exclaimed. "You'd think he was being led to the gallows."

"This is highly unusual," Evie said. "I don't blame anyone for feeling so on edge. It's hard to ignore the air of guilt and suspicion hovering in the air." Pouring another cup of coffee, she sat down.

The Dowager drew everyone's attention with nothing more than the sweep of her eyes around the room. "Isn't anyone going to comment on my remarkable piece of news?"

Bicky rang the bell and asked the under butler to organize someone to call on Hainsley Hall. "I would like a clear account. Gather as many facts as you can, please."

"I see," the Dowager harrumphed. "You refuse to take my word."

"With all due respect, mama. You provided a sketch of the events."

"But you didn't ask for more information," the Dowager pleaded. "I would have thought everything I said would be self-explanatory, but it seems you need a black and white picture with bright colors thrown in. Of course, I'll be only too happy to oblige."

Everyone in the room shifted and settled in for 'Act Two'.

Tom said, "If I'd known this would happen, I would have sold tickets at the door."

Unfortunately, Bicky sat within hearing. He exchanged a roll of the eyes look with Evie which reminded her of his opinions about Americans grasping every opportunity to make money.

To clarify his feelings, the Duke remarked, "Tom, you must give me private lessons on the art of entrepreneurship."

Before the Dowager could begin, Larkin appeared and called, "The Sergeant will now interview Lord Chambers."

Matthew adjusted his tie. "How do I look? I feel as though I'm about to interview for a position."

As he strode out, Viscount Maison entered the library and patted him on the back. "Good luck, old chap."

Everyone talked at once, asking Charles about the interview and expressing their surprise at how quickly it had gone for him.

"I'm afraid I'm not at liberty to divulge any details," Charles informed them. "The Sergeant wishes to receive personal perspectives and would prefer it if the information remained undiluted. You should all relax. He only had a few questions. Nothing too arduous."

After a moment's silence, the Dowager said, "May I be permitted to continue."

"By all means, mama. You have our full attention."

The Dowager gave a firm nod and continued her tale. "As I was saying, Miss Wainscot came close to losing her life." The Dowager paused for effect. "It appears Miss Wainscot had been lured by Evangeline Parker to *Marceline's Salon de Beaute*." Another pause followed. Then, the Dowager's voice lowered and filled with intrigue as she asked, "What do you all think of that?"

"Preposterous," Bicky thundered.

The room fell silent and everyone looked toward Evie.

Evie smiled as she remembered Bicky had been confined to his room at the time. "Actually, Bicky, the Duchess is quite correct... sort of. I did invite Miss Wainscot to take advantage of an appointment I had made at *Marceline's Salon de Beaute*." Evie made a point of lifting her chin. "But, I wish to be perfectly clear about this. I did not lure her."

"There, mama. Are you quite satisfied?" Bicky asked.

The Dowager looked confused. "It's not me she has to convince, but rather the authorities, the judge and the jury."

"Nonsense," Bicky said. "I'm sure this is nothing but a misunderstanding."

"Is it? But you have yet to hear the rest of the evidence against Evangeline Parker." The Dowager drew in a breath. "Upon subjecting herself to the beauty treatment, poor Miss Wainscot remained ignorant of what would happen next." The Dowager gave a sorrowful sigh. "Such a bright and beautiful girl in her full bloom, nipped in the bud by the nefarious machinations of a devious woman intent on clearing all obstacles from her path to her second matrimonial conquest."

Tom looked at Evie and murmured, "Is that so?"

"Not you too," Evie murmured back.

Tom grinned. "Haven't you heard? Majority rules and mob mentality prevails over all truth."

"If you are quite finished Mr. Winchester," the Dowager said, "I would like to resume my account of this creature's wicked assault on one of our own."

At this point, Evie couldn't tell if the Dowager

wanted to have fun at her expense or if she really meant what she said.

"Miss Wainscot now lies in the throes of agony, trying to overcome the damage caused to her by the products used on her delicate complexion. The girl has been disfigured by an attack of hives. All her prospects have been dashed. She is now a monster and will, most likely and forever more, live in the shadows of what might have been."

"Mama, I am sure you exaggerate," Bicky said. "Perhaps Miss Wainscot suffered a reaction."

"Yes. She did indeed suffer a reaction." The Dowager's voice hitched. "To poison."

CHAPTER 15

To the Gallows

$\mathcal{E}$vie swayed.

If Tom hadn't taken hold of her arm, she might have toppled over.

Poisoned?

Surely the Dowager had to be exaggerating. She had a great fondness for taking center stage and commanding an audience with her accounts. Usually, her stories revolved around the peculiarities of village life. Mostly, they were intended as a way to amuse.

"You should sit down," Tom suggested.

"Why do I get the feeling the plot has just thickened?" Looking up at Tom, she tried to anchor herself to the steadiness she saw in his eyes.

"It could be nothing more than coincidence," he said. "Or, perhaps Miss Wainscot did suffer a reaction."

"That can't be possible." Evie shook her head. "*Marceline's Salon de Beaute* provides an excellent service. They might be located in a small village, but they are part of a larger beauty product enterprise." Evie held her hand to her chest. "Do you think I might have been the intended target?" She didn't wait for him to answer. "Again? How could that be?"

Tom murmured, "We don't know that."

Evie turned and went to stand by the window; her hopes pinned on finding inspiration and clarity. She sensed Tom coming to stand beside her.

"When you asked me to wait for you by the village green, I saw a woman coming out of the store," Tom said. "She crossed the street but I noticed she kept glancing toward the store."

"Yes. Lotte Browning." Evie's heart gave a distinct thump of alarm. "I'm sure she heard me making the appointment." She gave him a brief rundown of everything she knew about Lotte Browning. "She's only a gossip. No harm done."

"Is that what you want to think or what you believe to be true?" Tom asked. "Push a person hard enough, and you'll be surprised what they can do."

Evie gave a pensive nod. "Lotte Browning has aspirations, if not for herself, then for her children. She'd never put that at risk. Think of the scandal such a devious action would cause. She'd never survive it. No, I don't really believe she had anything to do with this. Besides, what would she have done? Tampered with the product? How?" Although, she knew someone must have, Evie thought. But not Lotte Browning. "If I'm to suspect her of anything, it would have to be of sharing the information with someone who might then have taken steps to intervene."

Tom's eyebrows hitched up. "I think we might be going about this all wrong."

"What do you suggest we do?" Evie asked.

"We might need to sit down and make a list of all your enemies, including anyone who might harbor resentments." Tom brushed his hand across his chin. "What about the staff at the store?"

"Anna. I trust her implicitly. She's a wonderful girl. I can't imagine she would have any reason to cause me harm."

"Anyone else?" Tom asked.

"I can't say for sure. I assumed she would be the one in charge of giving treatments, but perhaps they have another employee." Evie shook her head. "So, until I can talk to her, there is simply no point in jumping to conclusions."

Tom handed her a cup of tea.

Evie smiled. "You're getting the hang of it." Evie took a

sip and decided to wait until they had more detailed information to go on with. "For the time being, I wish to believe this is nothing more than an unfortunate coincidence."

"Yes," Tom agree, "I'm thinking the same." Looking around the room, Tom mused, "Lady Charlotte seems to have a lot to say. She's been with the Sergeant longer than any of the others."

"It's not surprising," Evie remarked. "You know Charlotte's thoughts often meander. She actually possesses a fount of knowledge. Unfortunately, she doesn't always use it for good."

"Larkin," the Dowager said, "I should very much like a cup of tea now, please."

"Certainly, Your Grace."

"And bring a chair here please. I'd like to remain close to the door."

Tom chuckled and whispered, "It seems the Dowager is intent on making sure you do not make your escape."

Finally, Lady Charlotte returned, her cheeks slightly flushed. She resumed her seat next to her husband and, casting a furtive glance at Evie, she sighed.

Evie whispered, "I hope I'm not reading too much into it, but I get the impression Charlotte means to apologize to me."

"Whatever for?" Tom asked.

"I'm not sure yet. I guess I'll soon find out."

Larkin announced, "The Sergeant will now speak with the Countess of Woodridge."

Tom winked at her. "You're up."

The Sergeant began by apologizing, "Lady Woodridge, this can't be easy for you."

"I'm not the one with a wounded arm," Evie said. "I should like to help in any way I can. What would you like to know?"

"You could start by describing the moment immediately preceding the attempt on His Grace's life."

Evie recounted those few seconds. When she finished, she shifted to the edge of her seat thinking the Sergeant would thank her and move onto the next person.

She could not have been more wrong.

The Sergeant cleared his throat and asked. "Did you guide His Grace toward the window?"

Meaning what? "No, I... I had been seated next to Lady Charlotte." Evie gestured to the group of chairs behind her.

"And you then joined His Grace by the window."

"That's correct."

"What prompted you to move away at the precise moment you did?"

Evie's eyebrows drew down. "I didn't... Not exactly. I only turned to set down my teacup."

"Why did you do that? Had you actually finished your tea?"

"Well, no..."

The Sergeant held her gaze for a moment, his intention not quite clear to Evie. Although, she suspected he wanted to build anticipation and... suspense.

Finally, he asked, "So, why did you set your teacup down at the precise moment when a shot was fired at the Duke?"

"I had no control over the timing."

Her remark prompted the Sergeant to draw his eyebrows down.

Evie lifted her chin. "I set the teacup down because I had something to say to the Duke and I felt I needed to focus on the task."

"You felt holding the teacup would distract you?" he asked.

Evie gave a reluctant nod.

"Interesting," the Sergeant mused. He flipped through a few pages and then tapped his notebook. "Someone mentioned you had been glancing around you and that you looked slightly on edge." He checked his notebook. "In fact, you were described as looking rather anxious."

Evie bit the edge of her lip. She had been trying to determine how she could break the news to Bicky without alarming him too much or calling into question his absolute authority over his lands. Landowners took their responsibilities seriously and any mishaps on their property would be deemed a failure to take care of their own.

"I had been trying to break some news to His Grace and I didn't want anyone overhearing me."

"Is this something you can share with me?" the Sergeant asked.

"Yes, of course." Her chin lifted. "I have nothing to hide."

"Yet, you didn't want others to overhear you."

Evie jumped to her own defense. "Only because I didn't wish to alarm them. This is a house party and I feared the news might cast a shadow over the weekend." Drawing in a breath, Evie told the Sergeant about the incident on the road.

"When exactly were you going to report this to the authorities?"

"I shared the information with His Grace knowing he would then take the next step in deciding how best to proceed." Evie knew titled landowners carried a great deal of weight in such matters.

"But that didn't happen because he was then shot," the Sergeant mused.

"Well, as a matter of fact, I didn't get the chance to tell him until much later."

The Sergeant straightened. "Is there anyone else who can corroborate your story?"

"Story? Which story?"

"About the incident on the road," the Sergeant explained.

Evie straightened. "Isn't my word enough?"

"I only wish to get the facts straight," he said. "You were out on the road. Does that mean you were driving yourself?"

Evie tried to come up with a way to redirect the Sergeant's line of questioning. For the first time, she appreciated Lady Charlotte's talents. Some people had powers of persuasion, she excelled at digressing; deviating from the main conversation, sometimes losing the thread, deliberately or accidentally getting sidetracked and straying toward other subjects which may or may not have any relevancy to the main topic of conversation.

Having done a thorough job of distracting herself, Evie asked, "I'm sorry, what was the question again?"

"Were you driving yourself?" the Sergeant repeated.

"If I tell you, you'll have to promise to keep the information to yourself."

The Sergeant's eyebrows rose with interest. "Is this another secret?"

"Not exactly. However, it's not something I wish to share with everyone."

After a few moments, he nodded.

"My chauffeur's name is Tom."

The Sergeant scanned a list which Evie assumed contained the names of all the guests and quite possibly the household staff.

"And how might I contact him?"

"Is it absolutely necessary?" Evie asked. "He saw exactly what I saw."

"Perhaps, but we won't know for sure unless I speak with him."

Evie drew in a breath. "Tom Winchester..." Evie gestured to the Sergeant's list.

Acting on the prompt, the Sergeant's eyes dropped to his list. "I seem to have a Mr. Tom Winchester listed as a guest."

"That's correct."

The Sergeant sat up. His lips parted slightly. Drawing in a deep breath, he asked, "Your chauffeur shares the same name as one of the guests?"

Evie chortled. "That would be too much of a coincidence and quite unlikely."

"Are you saying your chauffeur..." He tapped his notebook, "Tom Winchester is also Mr. Tom Winchester, a guest at the Duke of Hetherington's house party?"

"It's rather a long story," Evie said.

The Sergeant settled back in his chair as if to suggest he had all the time in the world to hear it.

Evie emerged from the blue drawing room and pressed her hands to her cheeks. They felt hot to the touch. Looking up, she saw Tom approaching.

"I guess it's my turn," he said.

She couldn't escape the feeling of having betrayed their mutual cause. She couldn't keep the information to herself. Tom had to know. Evie whispered, "I had to tell him—" She heard the Sergeant clearing his throat.

Tom gave her a brisk smile. "This should be interesting."

Urged by the Sergeant, Tom strode into the blue drawing room. For a moment, Evie felt tempted to press her ear to the door, but then Larkin cleared his throat.

"It seems there is something going around. I hope it's not too serious or contagious, Larkin," Evie remarked as she strode past him and entered the library.

The Dowager spoke first, "I see. You remain a free woman."

Evie smiled at her. "According to the law, I am innocent until proven guilty."

The Dowager gave an unladylike snort. "One would think there is already sufficient evidence for you to be incarcerated."

To Evie's relief, the Dowager then winked at her.

Sinking into a chair, Evie tried to convince herself everything would work out. The police knew what they were doing and now they had a clearer picture of the events that had taken place.

"I hope the Sergeant recovered," Charlotte murmured.

"What do you mean?" Evie asked.

Charlotte lifted one eyebrow. "Well, as I related my tale, I had to prompt him several times because he appeared to look confused. It seems some people are ill equipped to follow a conversation."

The Dowager scoffed. "My dear, if you meandered along the way you usually do, then I'm not surprised at the Sergeant's confusion. You do tend to prattle on." The Dowager looked at Evie. "Did you manage to untangle him from his confusion?"

Up to a point, Evie thought. The news about Tom being both her chauffeur and a guest seemed to derail the Sergeant somewhat.

"He had no trouble understanding me." Evie turned to Charlotte. "By the way, what on earth did you tell him about me? He seemed to think I had set Bicky up to take the shot."

"And, did you?" the Dowager demanded.

CHAPTER 16

Hot on the trail

A walk and a breath of fresh air went a long way toward restoring Evie's optimism. The authorities would get to the bottom of this… whatever this was.

Hearing her name called out, she turned to see Tom striding toward her. Evie watched him, taking the sight of him in. Her breath stalled for a moment until she gave a brisk shake of her head and snapped herself out of the stupor.

"You disappeared." His face looked rather stern.

When he reached her, Evie noticed him looking at her as if he were making sure not a hair on her had been…

What?

Harmed?

"I needed to clear my head. Meaning, I couldn't stand to listen to another word, so I stepped out for a moment."

Tom appeared to relax, but his expression remained serious. "Next time, you might want to let me know."

"Why? Did you come close to raising the alarm?"

"I wouldn't joke about it." As he spoke, he looked around.

Evie smiled. "I think you'll find only birds, rabbits and foxes are out and about today."

He didn't appear to appreciate the remark. His attention remained on their surroundings. Had he only come out to perform his bodyguard duties? She'd been enjoying their easy-going exchanges and, while she knew most people would find it inappropriate, she wanted to think they could continue on this path.

"Tell me about your interview with the Sergeant. Did it go well?" she asked.

Tom nodded. "I found it quite straightforward. He seemed to be eager to stick to facts and somewhat relieved when I complied."

Evie shrugged. "That would have been easy enough to do if his questions required yes or no answers."

He studied her for a moment. "You seem to speak your mind. Did you do that at your interview?"

"I might have but only because the Sergeant seemed intent on reaching conclusions about me. Sometimes, it's best to get everything out into the open." She lifted her chin a notch. "So, were you at all helpful?"

"He will look into the incident on the road. But he wouldn't say if the two were related."

"They must be." Which meant... She had a target on her back.

He nodded. "Yes, I agree."

"What about Miss Wainscot? Did he mention her at all?"

Tom shook his head.

That meant the Dowager had been telling tales. It wouldn't be the first time she'd had fun at Evie's expense. "Has the Dowager Duchess left?" Evie asked.

"No, she's staying on for luncheon."

"Fabulous." Evie's tone lacked all enthusiasm, which said a great deal about how she felt. She always enjoyed the Dowager's teasing. Not so much today. "I've been thinking, I'd like to go into the village and see Anna."

"The girl who works at Marceline's Salon de Beaute?"

"Yes." Evie couldn't help smiling.

"Did I say it wrong?" Tom asked.

"No, as a matter of fact, you were spot on. I just... I never thought I'd hear those words spoken by you."

He gave a small nod of understanding. "I think I am what you might call a quick study."

"Yes, I've noticed. How did you pick up that particular trait?" she wondered out loud.

"I used necessity as a driving force. In the past, I've had to adjust to different circumstances..." He stopped, almost as if he'd realized he'd said too much.

He'd already hinted at having done a similar job, working as a bodyguard. As curious as she felt, Evie decided against pushing him for more information and assumed he would tell her more in his own good time. "Will you drive me into the village?"

His eyebrows rose. "You're actually asking me?"

Oh, she had.

Evie cleared her throat. "Tom, after luncheon, I'd like you to drive me to the village."

"Yes, ma'am."

Evie settled into the roadster next to Tom. "I've been thinking... I'd like to get a dog."

Tom glanced at her but didn't say anything. When they reached the gates to the estate, he stopped to watch for traffic, even though they were unlikely to encounter anyone, at least not until they reached the main road leading into the village.

"A dog?" he asked, his voice carrying a hint of humor.

Evie brightened. "Yes. I'm not sure why I haven't thought of it before."

"Have you ever owned a dog?"

"No. My mother is allergic. Now… Well, if she visits, I suppose I could keep Henry in another room."

"Henry?"

"You don't care for the name?" Evie asked. "How about Chester?"

"You might want to wait until you actually get a dog before bestowing a name on it."

"True. I suppose there is much to consider. I will make inquiries. Perhaps someone has a litter." She suddenly felt excited at the prospect. Clapping her hands, she added, "Oh, this could happen sooner than expected."

Tom chuckled. "Have you been thinking about it for a while?"

"No, the idea came to me now." Evie scanned the road and surrounding countryside. "If you must know, I'm trying to avoid feeling overly concerned about being out and about in a roadster, no less."

He gave a nod of understanding. "Do you normally distract yourself by making big life decisions?"

"I probably do, but I haven't noticed it until now." Evie decided to remain silent until they reached the village. Since she had used the idea of getting a dog to distract her from worrying too much about another possible attempt on her life, she now kept her mind engaged on trying to figure out what type of dog breed she would choose. "The more I think about it, the more I realize I will have to give it a great deal of thought."

They drove right up to Marceline's Salon de Beaute, along the way attracting the attention of everyone strolling around.

Holding the car door open for her, Tom asked, "Are you still thinking about getting a dog?"

"Indeed, I am."

"You might want to consider acquiring a guard dog," he suggested.

"Oh, I was actually thinking of something small I could pamper and carry around with me in a small basket or in my arms."

"So, rather than have the dog work for you, you wish to become a servant to your little master?"

Evie gave him an impish smile. "Or I could have you carry it."

Tom's expression firmed. Evie imagined he wanted to hide the dismay he felt. As they entered the salon, Evie couldn't help widening her smile. "I can already picture you with a cute little Pug. I hear the Prince of Wales is fond of them. If I ever meet him in person, we'll have something in common to talk about."

"Lady Woodridge," Anna greeted her.

Evie turned her attention to Anna and studied her expression. She didn't appear to be concerned about Evie's arrival. In fact, Anna's gaze shifted from one display to the next, probably trying to work out which one she would bring to Evie's attention first.

Without turning, Evie knew the precise moment when Tom came to stand a step behind her.

Anna's gaze shifted to Tom and stayed on him. Her eyes widened with appreciation and her lips curved just a little further.

"Anna, this is Mr. Tom Winchester."

Anna gave him a small nod. Eventually, she wrenched her eyes away from him. "How may I help you today, milady?"

"I wish to inquire about the appointment I made."

Anna's smile wavered. "Was there a problem with it, milady? I had the impression Miss Wainscot had been quite pleased with the service."

Strange, Evie thought. Anna hadn't expressed any surprise. "I hope it didn't cause an inconvenience for you. After all, I made the appointment for myself and then I took the liberty of offering it to someone else."

"Oh, that's perfectly fine, milady. In fact, we were very glad to be able to offer Miss Wainscot the service. I don't believe she has ever been here before. There is no better advertising than a happy customer referring another one to our salon."

Either Anna knew how to keep a poker face or she had no idea of Miss Wainscot's current state of misery.

"So, she was pleased with the service," Evie mused.

"Oh, yes. In fact, she took away one of our products

to maintain her beauty treatment." Anna looked over her shoulder and then back at Evie. "I shouldn't really be saying this, but we are trained to encourage our customers to try new products."

"What sort of product did she purchase?" Evie asked.

Anna smiled brightly. "A facial treatment, milady. It's a facial cream to maintain the skin looking youthful and vibrant."

Evie didn't wish to dispute the unethical promotion of a product that didn't really serve a purpose as, in her opinion, Miss Wainscot still had vibrant youth in her favor and would hardly need to reap the benefits of an expensive product to maintain her youthful glow.

Anna brought out her appointment book. "She was so pleased, she made another booking for herself in a month's time."

"How long does the treatment last for?" Tom asked.

"About an hour, sometimes longer. We never hurry our customers as the treatment is very relaxing. In fact, we encourage them to relax for a while after it is finished."

Long enough for something toxic to take effect, Evie thought. "I hope you don't find this odd. May I ask who provided the treatment?"

Anna blushed slightly. Leaning in, she whispered, "The regular girl called in sick so I had to do it myself."

"Is it a complex procedure?" Tom asked.

"Not at all but it does require expertise. It involves facial massages… techniques developed in Paris. We are fully trained. These products have been scientifically produced to provide exacting results," Anna explained, her tone sounding like a recitation she had learned by rote.

"What are some of the ingredients used?" Tom asked.

"There are some natural herbs and fragrances such as lavender, pine bark and water lilies."

"And do you prepare it yourself?" Tom asked.

Anna gave a swift shake of her head. "Oh, no. The cream comes in a sealed container to maintain its freshness and purity."

Sensing Tom's skepticism, Evie said, "Thank you, Anna. You have been most helpful."

As they strode out, Tom said, "You seemed to be satisfied with her responses and quite convinced of her innocence."

"Why shouldn't I be. Miss Wainscot left the premises a happy client."

"Out of curiosity, have you subjected yourself to these treatments?"

Evie lifted her chin slightly. "As a matter of fact, yes I have."

The edge of his eyes crinkled slightly. "And do you know what they put on your face?"

Evie tried to keep her voice light. "Of course, I do."

Tom stopped by the car and crossed his arms. "Tell me what the main ingredient is."

She didn't hesitate to say, "Lanolin."

He tilted his head in thought. "It sounds sufficiently scientific."

Evie tried not to smile. "It comes from sheep."

"How so?"

"If I tell you, will you promise not to mock the gullibility of women?"

His eyebrows curved upward. "Will I have reason to mock you?"

Evie gave it some thought. After hearing so much about the rise in success of the beauty industry, she had become intrigued. By 1915, Helena Rubinstein had set up her beauty salon in New York and when Evie had returned to America in 1918, she had made a point of meeting her. During the course of the conversation, she had delved into the process involved in making some of the products, absorbing as much information as she could in order to make a sound decision. At the time, she had been keen to invest in something other than the usual railways, shipping and stocks.

"Wool grease."

Tom held her gaze for a long moment before saying, "You put wool grease on your face."

"Of course not." She could not have sounded more shocked. "The raw ingredient is processed and blended with other essential and highly beneficial ingredients."

To his credit, Tom managed to keep a straight face.

Sighing, Evie looked around her. They now needed to speak with Miss Wainscot, but that could prove problematic.

The Dowager Duchess might have made up part of her story, embellishing it for the sake of entertainment, but Evie thought there might be some truth to it. In which case, she would be the last person Lady Wainscot wished to see.

"Well, we have managed to cross someone off our list, the one we have yet to put together," Evie said. "I only hope the guilty party doesn't beat us to it by taking action again before we've had the opportunity to identify them. That would be highly ungracious."

Tom barely contained his laughter. "Are you now trying to lighten the mood by being amusing?"

She wanted to say it always worked for the Dowager. Why shouldn't it work for her too? Sliding into the passenger seat, Evie stared straight ahead. "To quote the Dowager, the day manners become superfluous is the day society loses all meaning."

Tom took his place behind the wheel. Appearing to hesitate, he turned to Evie. "Did the Dowager Duchess really say that?"

"If she hasn't already said it, I'm sure given the opportunity, she will."

"In other words... You just made that up."

"Drive on, please."

CHAPTER 17

Eligible bachelors sacrificed for the greater good

Hainsley Hall, Lady Wainscot's residence.

𝓗ainsley Hall sat in a well-cared for park within only a few minutes of the village. Before setting out on their expedition, Evie had asked Bicky for directions, although she had silently prayed she could avoid a confrontation with Lady Wainscot.

"Are we likely to encounter a problem?" Tom asked as he drove through the gated entrance.

"Whatever do you mean?"

"I have come to understand the landed gentry don't really appreciate unexpected visitors landing on their doorstep."

"Nonsense. Everyone is welcoming."

"Really? Last night Charles and Matthew talked at length about Miss Wainscot's unexpected visit and the trouble you and Lady Charlotte went to in order to encourage Miss Wainscot's exit."

Evie waved her hand. "There are exceptions and that happened to be one of them. We knew Miss Wainscot had been sent to snoop around."

"And now you're going to return the favor."

Evie waited for Tom to come around her side and open the door before saying, "I am here to call on Lady Wainscot and inquire after her health as well as her daughter's. I'm sure she'll understand my concerns."

"You're not worried she'll accuse you of trying to permanently disfigure her daughter?"

Hard to say what Lady Wainscot would do, Evie thought. "I'm sure she'll be reasonable and understand I had nothing to do with her daughter's misfortune." Only if she employed the right tactic, Evie thought. The situation would call for extreme caution and delicacy.

Evie emerged from the car and stood toe to toe with him. "Could you please be a little more supportive and positive. We might be able to help her."

"Really? How so?"

Evie gave an impatient shrug. "Miss Wainscot left the Salon in perfect health. Either she stumbled into a poisonous shrub or someone tampered with the beauty therapy product. A few discreet questions might help us get to the bottom of this." And then, Evie thought, they could be free to focus on other matters such as her own wellbeing as well as Bicky's.

The butler announced them as, "The Countess of Woodridge and Mr. Winchester."

They entered the drawing room and found several people turning toward them, their eyes brimming with curiosity. Not one of them appeared to express any personal opinions. With any luck, Evie thought, they would only need to tackle one obstacle. She only hoped it didn't prove to be insurmountable.

"Lady Woodridge," Lady Wainscot clipped out. Dressed in severe black, she sat on a high-backed chair holding court over her guests whose attention swept toward her with such swiftness, Evie knew they didn't wish to miss any part of the exchange.

Time to bring out the rabbit from its hat, Evie thought. "Lady Wainscot. I have come to convey the Duke's well wishes for your daughter's speedy recovery. We were shocked to hear she had been taken ill."

Evie didn't know any of the half dozen or so people gathered in the drawing room so she couldn't vouch for their discretion. She didn't even dare to assume they would remain loyal to Lady Wainscot and keep everything they heard to themselves. In fact, she suspected they would use everything they heard to their advantage, stoking the fires for their own amusement and helping to spread the news about the encounter as a way of strengthening the animosity created by her ladyship's remarks.

She had no doubt Lady Wainscot had been the instigator of much of the gossip that had been making the rounds of the county. Under normal circumstances, Evie would have continued to keep her distance. The fact she had deemed it necessary to set foot inside Lady Wainscot's house spoke of desperation.

"The Duke knows of my daughter's illness?" Lady Wainscot asked. She appeared to have momentarily put aside her misgivings, her eyes brightening with interest. "And he has expressed his concern?"

"Yes, indeed." Evie smiled. "In fact, he is not the only one who expressed his concerns." Evie didn't normally employ underhanded tactics, but the current state of affairs called for them. "Viscount Maison took the news badly. I'm not sure if you know this, but he is the Earl of Braithwaite's heir."

Lady Wainscot gave a vigorous nod.

"Also, Mr. Mark Harper wanted to extend his best wishes for a speedy recovery."

A murmur swept across the drawing room.

"Mr. Harper, heir to his cousin, the Earl of Chatterlain?" Lady Wainscot asked.

Evie gave her a timid smile. "Yes, indeed. You know of him?" Evie would bet anything Lady Wainscot had memorized all the large estates of the area as well as the ones bordering Yorkshire and even beyond. She would also bet Lady Wainscot knew everyone's title and who stood in the line of succession, ready to take their place. In fact, she had no doubt Lady Wainscot kept an up to date copy of Burke's Landed Gentry on her bedside table or perhaps under her pillow, as well as the essential *Debrett's…*

Before Lady Wainscot could recover from the surprise of two such suitable candidates inquiring after her daughter, Evie said, "I understand Miss Wainscot took ill soon after her beauty treatment."

Lady Wainscot's eyebrows drew downward. "Soon after, yes."

It relieved her to realize the Dowager Duchess had been exaggerating. Lady Wainscot could not possible hold Evie responsible. Otherwise, she would have shown her the door. Either that or Lady Wainscot had managed to work off some of her unjustified anger toward Evie.

"And how is she now?"

Lady Wainscot dabbed the corner of her eye with her lace handkerchief. "In recovery but she may never be the same again. With all due respect, Lady Woodridge, you cannot know the pain I feel…" Lady Wainscot pressed her hand to her chest, "Seeing my eldest child denied the opportunity to shine during her season."

Her season? At twenty-five, Evie estimated this would be Miss Wainscot's fifth attempt to attract a suitable husband.

"I wonder... Would it be possible to speak with Miss Wainscot? As I said, the gentlemen were greatly concerned about her wellbeing." Evie smiled. "It might cheer her up to hear me say so." After casting the lure, Evie felt a twinge of guilt. Needs must, she thought.

Lady Wainscot took a second to think about it. Evie suspected she used the time to contain her bubbling excitement.

Two gentlemen concerned about her daughter's welfare. What could be better?

With a nod from her, the butler moved and gestured to the door. "If you would please follow me, My Lady."

Tom strode out with her but remained by the staircase.

Hainsley Hall appeared to have been built as a homage to larger estates. It had all the comforts of a large country manor, albeit on a more modest scale. The Wainscot ancestors all peered down at Evie as she made her way up the stairs. They reached the landing and then strode past a couple of suits of armor standing guard over the family's private rooms.

The butler opened a door and stepped aside.

Despite it being the middle of the afternoon, the room remained in darkness with only a sliver of light daring to infiltrate the gloom.

A light moan guided Evie toward the four-poster bed. As Evie's eyes adjusted to the dark, she saw Miss Wainscot lying on the bed, her face covered with a veil.

"Wilfred? Is that you?" Clarissa Wainscot asked, her voice lacking the vibrancy of the day before.

"Yes, Miss Clarissa. You have a visitor," the butler said.

"Wilfred, you know I'm in no fit state to receive visitors."

Before the butler could speak, Evie said in a soft murmur, "It's Lady Woodridge. I have come to see if there is anything I can do for you."

After a moment's hesitation, Miss Clarissa said, "Thank you, Wilfred. That will be all."

"Very well, Miss Clarissa."

Evie waited for the butler to withdraw before saying, "How are you feeling?"

Miss Clarissa made a choking sound. "My life is ruined. I am disfigured."

"News about your illness has caused great distress at Yarborough Manor. Everyone is concerned about your wellbeing."

"Really?" the news seemed to brighten Miss Clarissa.

"Yes. Viscount Maison and Mr. Harper were particularly concerned about you."

Miss Clarissa made an effort to sit up. "The doctor assures me I will recover within a few days."

Evie barely managed to hide her relief. "Our prayers have been answered. We have all been hoping for a speedy recovery."

Miss Clarissa could not have sounded more surprised. "You have?"

"Yes, of course."

"How kind of you to say so. I had no idea I had made such an impression on Viscount Maison or Mr. Harper." The veil slipped away from her face revealing red blotches on her cheeks, chin and forehead. Miss Clarissa gasped and adjusted the veil back in place. "You must think me a monster."

"Nonsense." Evie edged closer to the bed. "Does it hurt?"

"Not at all," Miss Clarissa assured her. "I'm afraid my eyes are puffy. Until this morning, I thought I would die."

Evie patted her hand. "I spoke with Anna at *Marceline's Salon de Beaute*. She assured me you were quite content with the treatment."

Miss Clarissa gave a small nod.

"What happened?"

"Soon after I arrived home, I felt sleepy so I took a nap."

Evie remembered she had felt the same way after her treatment and had been told it had been the result of the relaxing therapy.

"When I woke up, my face felt itchy and sore."

"How dreadful," Evie exclaimed.

"I could barely breathe."

Evie thought she must have panicked and been beside herself with fear. "Did you happen to apply any of the cream you purchased?"

"No. I'd only just had the treatment so there was no need for it."

Perhaps the cream used for the treatment had been slow to take effect. Or...

"Do you still have the cream you purchased?" Evie asked.

Miss Clarissa nodded. "I set it down... somewhere."

"Do you mind if I look around for it?"

"Not at all, but... why do you want to see it?"

"Curiosity." Evie strolled around the room and stopped by the dresser where the brushes and several small pots were organized in neat rows. She held a pot up and asked, "Is this is?"

"I can't see very well from here, but it looks like it."

Evie went to stand by the window and shifted the thick velvet curtain enough to be able to read the label on the pot. Nodding, she said, "Yes, this is it." She twisted off the cap and peered inside. An indentation in the cream suggested some of it had been used. Evie smelled it. If someone had contaminated it with something toxic, it had not affected the light flowery fragrance. Only one way to know for sure, she thought and dabbed some on her hand. "You say you didn't use it at all."

"No, I didn't."

Well. Someone had.

Evie found Tom studying a painting of a severe looking Wainscot ancestor.

"Well?" he asked.

Evie looked toward the drawing room. She knew she should take her leave and thank Lady Wainscot for allowing her to see her daughter but, in all honesty, she simply didn't have the energy or patience to tackle that particular mountain.

Good sense won out and, scooping in a breath, she strode back into the drawing room to thank Lady Wainscot and report that the news had been well received and Miss Wainscot had cheered up considerably.

With a nod to the butler, Evie nudged Tom and they strode out. Outside, she gazed across at the garden. She hadn't noticed a young girl in the drawing room. She assumed Miss Clarissa's sister would be younger than twenty-five…

"Let's take a stroll around," she suggested.

"You're being mysterious," Tom said.

"My apologies. I didn't mean to be." Evie told him about her visit with Miss Clarissa.

"She went to sleep and then woke up with a rash?" Tom asked.

"That's right. And the cream she had purchased at *Marceline's Salon de Beaute* had been opened." Evie stopped and held up her hand.

"What am I looking at?"

"I dabbed some on. If there had been something toxic in the cream, my skin would have reacted to it. Look. It's perfectly fine."

"Maybe the cream contains a substance you're not allergic to," Tom suggested.

True. Miss Wainscot's rash had looked severe. However, Evie knew for a fact the cream only contained a basic herb. "What if someone else introduced a toxic substance? The container had been opened but Miss Wainscot said she hadn't used any. She went to sleep and then woke up with a rash."

"I guess you're now suggesting someone applied the cream after she fell asleep."

Evie nodded. "It is a possibility and the only one I can think of. They must have mixed something toxic into the cream. Perhaps they used something else to mix it in. Something easily obtainable." They strode toward a walled garden. Easing the gate open, they saw a small wilderness area. "Let's take a look around."

"Who and why?" Tom murmured.

After they circled around the garden a couple of times, Evie was about to suggest taking a walk outside the walled garden when she pointed to the far corner where a large majestic oak stood surrounded by bushes.

The path narrowed and the bushes appeared to be growing out of control. A wheelbarrow, rake and gardening implements had been left by the tree suggesting someone might be in the process of working in the area.

Evie stopped at the edge. "I think this is as far as I go. You have trousers."

"Yes, I do."

"Well, go on," Evie urged.

He gave her a blank look.

Evie gestured with her hand toward the large tree.

"You want me to trudge through the bushes in search of what?"

"Something toxic." Evie stood on her toes. "There. I see something right up against the wall and well away from the path."

Tom made his way to it. She watched him inspect the plant, look toward her and then back at the plant. A moment later, he returned.

"Stinging nettle," he said.

Evie's eyebrows shot up. "That's it. It has to be. Did you see if any of it had been cut off?"

"Yes."

Hearing the crunch of footsteps along the pebbled path, Evie turned. A young woman strode along the path and appeared to be headed toward a bench. When she saw Evie, she hesitated. Then, she turned and hurried away.

"Wait," Evie called out.

Instead of stopping, the young woman broke into a run.

"Tom, go after her."

As he hurried past her, Evie thought she heard him mutter something about telling him to fetch.

CHAPTER 18

Yarborough Manor

"Miss Eugene Wainscot," Evie announced as she strode into the Duke's drawing room, her voice conveying the euphoric triumph she felt.

Everyone set their cups down and gave Evie their full attention.

"She is the younger Miss Wainscot," Evie explained. "And she is the culprit."

"Well, that is one mystery solved," Bicky declared. "But, how did you discover her involvement?"

Evie sat down and related the story. "When Tom caught up with her, she burst into tears. She had guilt written all over her. As we asked questions, we learned the Honorable Miss Wainscot can cry on command. She eventually told us her sister had been insufferable. Since returning with the news about the beauty treatment and Charlotte's offer to sponsor her season, she had been talking about it non-stop and showing off to Miss Eugene. So, Miss Eugene decided to do something about it. She mixed some of the cream with stinging nettle and applied it while her sister slept."

Jealousy and malice. Pure and simple.

Evie looked around the drawing room. "Where's the Dowager Duchess?"

"She left soon after you did," Bicky said. "She'll be sorry to have missed the news."

"I doubt it since it puts me in the clear." Evie accepted a cup of tea and took a sip. "I've never seen her enjoying herself so much at my expense."

Tom settled down beside her to eat his fruitcake.

"Did you tell Miss Eugene's mama about her daughter's cruel antics?" Lady Charlotte asked.

"Tom felt we should but I really didn't want to stoke the fire. From what Miss Eugene said, her sister can be quite viciously competitive as well as cunning and cruel. Apparently, the previous year, Miss Clarissa had given her young sister a severe rash by sprinkling dried Baby's Breath on all her bed linen. I had no idea it could cause a rash. Anyhow, the rash cleared after a couple of days but she had not been fit to attend a significant ball in town."

Bicky strode around the room. "I don't quite understand why Lady Wainscot pointed the finger at you. Mama can be creative, but not to that extent."

Charlotte piped in, "It's common knowledge. Lady Wainscot holds a grudge against Evie for marrying Nicholas. I imagine she sees her as a threat now because Evie is, once again, available."

Bicky shook his head. "But that doesn't make sense. Lady Wainscot's daughters were not even out of the school room when Evie married."

Charlotte shrugged. "I suppose Evie instilled fear into every mama's heart. If one American heiress could sweep in and take the prize, then others might follow. Also, she is once again eligible and free to marry."

Mark Harper winked at Evie. "Perhaps you should set her mind at ease and announce your engagement to Mr. Winchester."

Evie had to remind herself Mark didn't actually know Tom Winchester and Mr. Tom Winchester were one and the same.

Glancing over at Tom, she wondered if it would make a difference. If she fell in love with a man, would she talk herself out of it simply because he was her social inferior?

"You're looking very serious," Charlotte remarked.

Bicky's sister, Elizabeth agreed. "That is her thinking look. Do share."

"Well, there is still the question of the attempt on Bicky's life." Evie thought it would be easier to stick with that theory. As far as she could remember, the others didn't know about the incident on the road.

"Oh," Elizabeth said. "I thought you might have been worried about still being a target."

Belatedly, Evie remembered Bicky had confided in his sister.

"What's this?" Penelope asked. "Why would Evie be a target?"

Lady Penelope rarely spoke up, unless she had something to complain about. So, when she did, she took Evie by surprise. So much so, Evie felt her cheeks flush as she realized she hadn't even noticed Lady Penelope sitting beside Elizabeth. This delayed her reaction, so she missed her opportunity to stop Elizabeth.

"Someone tried to kill Evie out on the road when she arrived yesterday," Elizabeth explained.

Penelope gasped. "Really?"

"Who would want to do that?" Charlotte asked. Looking at her empty plate, she got up and strode to the table to help herself to some cake. "This is unacceptable. Are we to be murdered in our beds?"

Elizabeth laughed. "Are you being serious or just quoting Mrs. Bennett?"

"Both. What if we're next? Someone might be trying to pick us off one by one until they succeed in getting rid of the lot of us." Realizing she stood close to the window, Charlotte hurried back to her seat. "Well, Duke? What assurance can you give us? Are we safe or not?"

Bicky nodded. "I'd say we are. Everyone is on the lookout for suspicious looking characters. No one would dare make another attempt on any of our lives."

"What are we to do for the remainder of our stay?" Charlotte asked. "I'm sorry to say, I don't buy into your confidence. I don't have the courage to set foot outside."

Lady Penelope agreed. Until now, she had kept her opinions to herself. Clearly, she now saw herself included in the threat.

For some reason, everyone turned to Tom. He must have sensed it because he looked up.

"I'm sorry, did I miss something?" he asked.

"We're looking to you for an answer," Penelope said.

He took a bite of his cake and after he swallowed, asked, "An answer to what?"

"This threat. What are we to do?" Charlotte asked.

After some thought and another bite of cake, Tom said, "I suggest we remain calm and start working on a list. Since the only victims so far are Bicky and Evie, we might want to focus on what they have in common."

"Larkin," Bicky said.

"Yes, Your Grace."

"Could we please have some pen and paper?"

"Certainly, Your Grace."

Charlotte looked from Bicky to Evie. "I say, you two wouldn't be trying to pull the wool over our eyes?" Her eyebrows drew downward. "Would you?"

"Whatever do you mean?" Evie asked.

"Pretending you were shot at on the road, that's what I mean."

"Why would we do that?"

"Because you and Bicky have decided to make this a mystery weekend. It's a fabulous idea, but I'd like to know if my life is truly in danger or not. I would prefer to know so I could have more fun playing the game."

Evie smiled. "Would you? I think it would be more realistic if you really believed your life hung in the balance." She gave Charlotte a moment to consider the idea. "However, we wouldn't be so cruel."

Charlotte could not have looked more disappointed.

Evie laughed. "If I didn't know better, I'd say you object to not being a target. In any case, Bicky has a wound on his arm. That cannot be ignored."

Charlotte glanced over at Bicky. "Of course. I'd... I'd forgotten."

Larkin appeared with the writing paraphernalia which included several fountain pens and notebooks.

"Perhaps one person could take notes while we hash it all out," Bicky suggested.

Despite Penelope putting her hand up and volunteering to take notes, Evie asked Larkin for a pen and paper. It had all started with being shot at on the road so she uncapped her pen and put her name at the top of the list.

Prime target. She then added Bicky's name alongside hers.

Looking at Tom, she wondered if perhaps he should be on the list too. Maybe someone had mistaken Bicky for him when they'd taken a shot at him through the drawing room window. Although, that didn't exactly make sense. No one would have expected her chauffeur to be inside the house.

"Who would like to go first," Charlotte asked. "No one? Fine, I'll put myself forward."

Evie didn't bother holding her laughter. Charlotte had clearly been keen to be heard, so she didn't give anyone else a chance to respond.

Looking over at Bicky, Charlotte gave him an apologetic look. "I think the Dowager Duchess has finally cracked it."

It took a moment for everyone to realize Charlotte must have been trying to lighten the mood. In any case, she went ahead and laughed.

"Honestly, you should see your faces. Filled with utter astonishment that the idea would even come to me. The Dowager Duchess is so many things. A killer? No, I don't think so."

Evie tapped her pen against her notebook. Bicky had been having issues of infidelity with his wife. Evie looked around her. The wife who had as yet to put in an appearance. "Has Clara not arrived?"

Bicky looked at the clock. "No, not yet. If she has, she's gone straight to her room. Although, if she had, Larkin would have informed me."

"Should we add Clara to the list of suspects?" Charlotte asked. "She is making herself obvious by her absence."

"And what possible motive would she have?" Elizabeth asked.

If anyone knew of Bicky's troubles, his sister would. However, Elizabeth had never once said a bad word against her sister in law.

Everyone in the room fell silent. It became obvious they all knew Bicky had been navigating troubled waters but they didn't want to make them murky by speaking ill of his absent wife.

It seemed Charlotte had no such qualms about airing her opinions.

Charlotte shifted. "Well, with Bicky out of the way, Clara would get her money back and she would be free to marry again."

Evie looked at Bicky. Instead of looking shocked or insulted by the insinuation his wife had been involved in the shooting, he looked rather pensive. Had Charlotte's remark touched a sore spot? He couldn't be entertaining the possibility. Surely not…

"But her money must be all tied up," Evie reasoned.

Bicky glanced at her. The small shake of his head suggested there might be something to Charlotte's accusation.

Tom leaned in and whispered, "Who is Clara?"

Evie murmured, "The Duchess of Hetherington. Bicky's wife. She's been away in London." Tapping her notebook, she asked, "I don't mean to draw attention to myself, however, does anyone know if I have any real enemies?"

Penelope and Elizabeth looked anywhere but at Evie.

"You must have," Charlotte said. "Some mamas have long memories."

Yes, but would any of them be prepared to wield a rifle? "I refuse to be held responsible for falling in love," Evie declared. "Besides, my success in the marriage stakes can't possibly be a motive. I am received everywhere."

"Of course, you are, dear." Elizabeth leaned forward and patted her hand. "Everyone is waiting to see what you will do next. They wouldn't dare deprive themselves of the performance. The first time you met Nicholas, you both had eyes for no one else. We might all have become invisible for all you cared. I'd give anything to see that again."

Evie's mouth gaped open. She'd never in a million years consider that as a reason for receiving so many invitations. Turning to Bicky, she couldn't help asking, "Is that why you have me over?"

"Nonsense. I'd like to think this is your haven where you can get away from all that silliness."

"And yet this is where someone made an attempt on my life." Evie rose to her feet and sought out the comfort of the window. Although, rather than stepping right up to it, she maintained a safe distance, hopefully out of sight of a would-be shooter.

"Could we please focus?" Charlotte asked. "The sooner we get to the bottom of this the sooner we can put ourselves in the clear as targets. I am honestly not comfortable with any of this."

Charlotte's husband, Lord Chambers, said, "My dear, I am on my way to becoming a peer and therefore a sitting member of the House of Lords. If you didn't know it already, I'm sorry to say but we have been targets for a very long time."

Charlotte visibly gulped.

Lord Chambers looked at Evie. "You have recently returned from America. Is it possible someone might have followed you here?"

Bicky sidled up to Evie and murmured, "He might have a point. After all, you now travel with a bodyguard pretending to be your chauffeur... and currently pretending to be your friend, or perhaps more than that, if the rumors are anything to go by."

"The rumors? Oh, you mean the ones spread by your mama?"

"Sometimes, I think she would fare better living in town," Bicky remarked. "She needs stimulation. I'm afraid she's always found her life in the country somewhat limited."

Evie looked over her shoulder to make sure no one but Bicky would hear her. "Bicky... Do you think there might be some truth to what Charlotte insinuated?"

He didn't need any explaining. Bicky laughed.

"I know," Evie said. "It's silly to suspect Clara."

"Silly?" he laughed again. "Oh, no. I'm laughing because you think Charlotte only insinuated it. She could not have been clearer and perhaps even spot on."

CHAPTER 19

In the dead of night...

"**W**hy the secrecy?" Tom whispered. "Couldn't we have asked to see the room?"

Evie put her finger to her lips and held up the candle. She knew Larkin made the rounds to check doors and windows precisely one hour after the last guest left or retired for the evening. It had always been his habit and would remain so until the day he ceased to be a butler.

All the guests had gone to their respective rooms an hour before and Evie had already heard Larkin's nightly vigil along the corridor. So, the way would be clear.

"Follow me," she said in a hushed tone.

Clara, Duchess of Hetherington, had not returned from her trip. According to Bicky, she had telephoned to say she had missed her train. However, Evie didn't recall hearing the telephone ringing at any time during the evening.

Their dinner had been filled with more suppositions about Evie's enemies. Bicky had insisted he couldn't be a target and everyone had concurred, murmuring they would be hard pressed to find anyone who didn't like him. By the end of it, everyone had managed to have a say. Although, most of the suggestions had sounded ludicrous.

Everyone had then decided Bicky had simply been in the wrong place. That could only mean, Evie had been the real target. Not once, but twice.

She did not for a moment believe all the mamas from across all the English counties had joined forces to have her run out of the country.

Nevertheless, she'd had no idea her life had been filled with so much peril. According to some, she might be snatched at anytime and anywhere and held for ransom.

It seemed extraordinary. The thought had never occurred to her. Or maybe, she had been aware of the possible risks involved but had never made a big deal out of it.

How stifling would it be to always wonder if today would be the day when something dreadful happened to her?

They continued along the corridor until they reached the family wing. Tom walked beside her. She sensed him but she didn't hear him. Evie had chosen to wear her slippers but she still walked with the greatest care. Tom, however, still wore his shoes and she knew for a fact some of the floorboards creaked. Yet, he managed to avoid them.

When they reached the room she wanted, she tugged his sleeve. Checking to make sure no one had seen them, Tom eased the door to the room open. Evie hurried inside, followed by Tom who then closed the door.

Once inside, she found the light switch and blew out her candle.

"Is that a good idea?" Tom asked.

Instead of answering, Evie grabbed a couple of cushions and placed them on the floor to cover the gap by the door. "Better?" she asked.

"Marginally." He strode to the windows and made sure the thick velvet curtains were drawn properly.

She glanced around the Duchess's room, cringing slightly at all the gold decorations. Even the cushions were embroidered with gold thread and embellished with gold tassels.

"There could be a hiding place," Evie suggested. They had already decided they needed to find some sort of proof against the Duchess. Anything that might give rise to suspicion and perhaps incriminate her in a plan to get rid of Bicky.

The others might have been content to strike him off the target list, but not Evie...

They had no solid reason to be suspicious of the Duchess. At this point, she supposed they were working on a process of elimination. If the Duchess was innocent, then they wouldn't find anything. Evie kept the thought to herself for fear Tom would find a hole in her theory. She could already sense one taking shape in her mind, but she preferred to leave it alone.

At Evie's insistence, they hadn't shared the plan with Bicky. In her opinion, Bicky had probably suffered enough. She had no doubt he had.

Clara had never pretended to care much for him. While Bicky had held on to the hope he might grow on her, saying his parents hadn't been in love at first, yet they had learned to appreciate one another and eventually they had fallen in love.

Tom opened a wardrobe door and, to Evie's surprise, he leaned in and smelled the coats. Tiptoeing her way to him, she asked, "What are you doing? Is this some sort of fetish?"

"I'm smelling her clothes to see if I can pick up a man's fragrance."

Even if they found traces of it, Bicky would never act on it. He would certainly never consider divorce. It simply wasn't done. There were cases but few and far between among their rank. Although, she had heard a rumor about the Duke of Marlborough's marriage heading that way, and perhaps it would be for the best since Consuelo Vanderbilt had left him in 1906.

"I think we might be wasting our time," Evie whispered. If only they could find something substantial like letters exchanged between lovers. They might even find something that could be interpreted as collusion... Some sort of conspiracy to do away with Bicky. Even a wishful thought captured on paper might lead them along the right track.

Tom abandoned the hope of finding a man's fragrance on Clara's coats and began searching through the drawers. They had already discussed the issue of privacy and had dismissed it as inconsequential. Far too much remained at stake for them to be sensitive to the Duchess's sensibilities.

Moments later, he drew Evie's attention by tapping her on the shoulder and holding up a box of matches. Pocketing it, he moved onto the mattress and searched under it.

Evie found a leather bound book on a bedside table.

She peered between the small gap in the spine and flipped through the pages but found nothing.

They had searched the entire room and had only found a box of matches which might or might not prove to be useful.

Could they cross Clara off the list of suspects?

Bringing their search to an end, they made sure they had left everything as they'd found it before leaving the room and heading back to Evie's room.

If Caro knew she had invited Tom into her bedchamber, Evie would... Well... she would definitely have a lot of explaining to do to her lady's maid.

Tom drew the matches out of his pocket. "It's from the Criterion. Do you know it?"

"Yes. It's in Piccadilly Circus. It's quite an opulent restaurant and bar."

"Would it be the type of place the Duchess would be seen in?" Tom asked.

"Yes, absolutely." Evie wondered if the Duchess had gone there by herself or if she used the fashionable restaurant as a rendezvous point.

"She kept the matches hidden in the back of the drawer wrapped in a handkerchief."

A sure sign she hadn't wanted anyone to see the box. But why?

Were the matches a keepsake? A memento from her first rendezvous with her lover who might, this very moment, be plotting to kill Bicky so he could have Clara all to himself?

Tom pocketed the matches. "Well, I suppose that's that. We can't point the finger of suspicion at the Duchess because she chooses to dine at a fine establishment."

He couldn't, but Evie had no qualms about reinstating the Duchess as a suspect.

Evie sat down at her dresser and opened the notebook she had used earlier. "I don't recall you making any suggestions."

He leaned against the wardrobe. "I've only been in your employ for a short time and you've mostly been keeping to yourself, stepping out of the house only once or twice a week."

"You could take a wild stab."

"There are seven house guests. I assume you knew them before coming here."

Evie nodded. "I've only met Mark Harper a couple of time but I've known the others for years. There's no reason why Mark would want to hurt me or scare me." He wouldn't have anything to gain.

Evie looked up at the ceiling. What if the shooter didn't have a motive? He might only be targeting the landed gentry for sport.

"Are all the ladies married?" Tom asked.

"Yes. They don't always travel with their husbands.

And, before you ask, I have never given any of them reason to be jealous."

"Are you sure?"

Evie subjected herself to close scrutiny. Bicky remained the only man she ever had murmured conversations with. She spoke to the others with ease but she honestly couldn't fault her behavior toward them. Although...

The Viscount and Mark Harper had recently teased her. However, their flirting still remained within acceptable boundaries.

"Even if I had my doubts, no one actually knew I'd be attending this house party. So, they could not have planned their assault on me."

"Which brings us back to my earlier suggestion," Tom said. "Someone must have been keeping an eye out for you."

Evie surged to her feet and insisted, "But no one knew I would be here." Drawing in a breath, she got herself under control.

"No one that you know of. What about your house-hold staff in town? Do you trust them all implicitly? How do you know someone didn't pay them to pass on information to let them know of your departure? The arrangement might have been made the last time you came here." He looked at her for a long moment. Finally, he said, "It's late. We'll talk about it some more in the morning."

Evie nodded. "If I make it to morning." She turned and looked at her bed. Holding up a finger, she rushed to the bed and pulled back the covers.

"Looking for bed bugs?" he asked.

"At this stage... I have no idea what I'm looking for. But I feel I should now grow eyes on the back of my head."

"That's why I'm here." He turned to leave, only to say, "Maybe getting a dog isn't such a bad idea."

CHAPTER 20

A wild goose chase...

"There's a telegram for you, Lady Penelope." Larkin bowed his head and handed her the envelope.

"Thank you, Larkin."

Evie made eye contact with Tom and gestured toward Penelope. A series of exchanged eyebrow movements later and Tom, who sat next to Penelope, reluctantly leaned in. However, at that precise moment, Penelope finished reading the message. Folding it, she slipped it inside its envelope.

"Good news, I hope," Evie said.

"No, I'm afraid not." Penelope took a long sip of her

coffee. "It is so disappointing when people let you down."

And yet... She didn't look disappointed. Glancing at Tom, Evie tried to interpret his slightly raised eyebrow look. "Don't leave us hanging."

"Oh," Penelope sighed. "It's nothing really. I devoted a great deal of my time to selecting a new wardrobe for the season and now my dressmaker tells me nothing will be ready on time. This is such a letdown. Of course, I will not be using her services again."

"She must have had a very good reason," Evie remarked. Although, in her opinion, once a promise had been made and delivery dates agreed upon, it would be in her best interest to satisfy her customer.

"Perhaps, but she didn't offer one. I shall now have to rush to town and make other arrangements. This is such an inconvenience and the timing could not have been worse. How can I possibly leave when your lives are still in danger?"

"We'll try to keep ourselves alive while you're away," Bicky offered.

"I wouldn't want you to think I'm bailing out on you." Penelope looked at him, her eyes expressing her gratitude. "Do you think I could be driven to the station?"

"Yes, of course. Larkin will see to it."

Excusing herself, Lady Penelope left on her rescue mission.

"Remind me again who she is," Tom whispered.

"Penelope is married to the eldest son of the Earl of Remington, which means she will one day be a Countess."

"Not any time soon," Bicky remarked. "The Earl enjoys extremely good health. That's not to say Penelope resents him for it. Did that sound odd?" Bicky didn't wait for anyone to respond. "I think it did sound rather odd and it might have to do with my growing cynicism about marriage." Looking around the table, he apologized. "I hope I haven't ruined your breakfast."

Mark Harper set his newspaper down. "No worse than what we read every morning. I suppose happy stories don't sell newspapers."

"As the eldest son of an Earl myself," Matthew, Lord Chambers, mused, "I don't think you are being cynical, Bicky. I'm sure I've been accused of champing at the bit but I'm in no hurry to step into my father's shoes and Charlotte is quite content to spend the time honing her skills. It's no easy task being at the helm of a large household. Wouldn't you agree, Evie?"

"I can't really say. Nicholas had already been an Earl when I married him. I had no choice but to jump in at the deep end." And, if anyone had resented her advantageous marriage, they had certainly not taken any drastic steps. Belatedly, she wondered if Matthew had meant to steer the subject away from unfaithful spouses. She would swear Bicky had meant to imply as much when he'd referred to his cynicism.

"Would anyone care to go out riding today?" Bicky asked.

Both Matthew and Mark accepted the invitation just as Charles, Viscount Maison, strode in and helped himself to some breakfast.

"Count me in," Charles said. "We'll be moving targets, so we should be fine."

Bicky looked at Evie and Tom. "Will you be joining us?"

Evie hadn't made any definite plans for the day but she didn't want to commit to a horse ride without first discussing their lack of success during the previous night's search with Tom. "We'd love to. However, I have some errands to run. In fact, the sooner we get started, the better."

"They must be important errands," Matthew observed.

"To me, yes." Evie gave him a brisk smile. "I'm keen to find out if anyone has a new litter."

"You're looking for a dog?" Bicky asked.

"Yes, I might be. I'm sure I want one. Actually, I think I should have one. I don't know why it never occurred to get one before."

"Because your mother suffers from allergies," Tom reminded her.

"Oh, yes… That's right." Evie looked around the

table. "I always try to avoid pointing the finger of blame at my mother for fear I might come across as being ungrateful."

"I will ask around for you," Bicky offered. "Someone is bound to be looking to place their puppies in a good home."

"Thank you."

"Well, since the rest of the ladies have yet to make an appearance, I'll wait for final numbers before sending word to the stables," Bicky said. "Will you be joining us for dinner?"

Evie looked at Tom, although she had no idea why she did so. "Yes, of course. We'll be here." It suddenly occurred to ask, "Are we likely to hear back from the Sergeant?"

Bicky nodded. "I trust the local authorities will inform us of any new developments."

Charles snorted. "I only hope there are some of us left to hear the news."

"You're looking pensive," Evie said as they strode out to the roadster.

Tom gave a small shrug. "Yesterday I suggested trying to determine what you have in common with Bicky. We never got around to figuring that out."

Evie slipped her leather gloves on and adjusted her

hat. "You're right. We didn't get very far with that. I remember I'd been obsessed with something Charlotte said about Clara." And that had led her to suggest they search her room for anything that might serve as evidence. Evie shook her head. "I'm still thinking about Clara. What if she's up to something?" Evie almost wished that were true. Bicky certainly deserved better.

"Aren't Dukes supposed to have children?" Tom asked.

"They sure are. The more, the better. Or, at least, as Consuelo Vanderbilt put it, an heir and a spare. Preferably male. You heard the Dowager Duchess. If anything happens to Bicky, his cousin thrice removed inherits."

They both stopped and stared at each other.

"It would be unthinkable," Evie remarked.

"But not impossible. What do you know about the heir?"

"Alexander Fleshling," Evie murmured.

"That's it? His name?"

"Give me a moment. I'm thinking out loud. I have met him. Bicky had him over before I returned to America. There had been another heir ahead of him, but he died during the war. If I remember correctly, he fell off his horse and broke his neck. Anyhow... Usually, with heirs so far removed, you tend to find they are ensconced in some sort of profession, medicine or the law, because they have to make a living." She tilted her head up as if seeking divine inspiration.

But nothing new came to her. "We'll have to ask Bicky. I'd be surprised if he's even kept in regular touch. He's still young."

Tom leaned against the motor car and stared at her. "Do you really have errands to run?"

"I do now. I'd like to know what was in Penelope's telegram."

"I guess you have reason to believe she hid the true contents from you."

The Penelope she knew would have shown her the telegram and made a big deal out of it. Instead, it had been folded and returned to the envelope as if for safe-keeping.

"So, how do you propose going about it?" Tom asked.

"I suppose it wouldn't hurt to stop by the telegraph office. The post mistress is rather lovely." Seeing Tom's eyes widening as if in disbelief, Evie rolled her eyes. "I see, you're not in favor of the idea."

Tom brushed his hand across his chin. "I'm curious to know how you would convince a post mistress to reveal what is possibly confidential information. I'm sure there is some sort of law or code of conduct in place about such things."

"Well, then... Perhaps we should drive to London and go to the Criterion. Who knows, if we sit there long enough we might encounter the Duchess and if we're really lucky, we might overhear a plot to do away with Bicky."

"That sounds like a plan. If we leave right now, I'm sure we'll arrive before lunch."

"In case you're wondering, yes, I am surprised to hear you agree with me. Don't you find the idea of the Duchess being somehow responsible rather ludicrous." Evie had already crossed her off the list because she didn't believe Clara would risk her freedom but she kept finding reasons for suspecting her again...

Tom shrugged. "Women in love have been known to do bizarre things."

"Did you feel that strongly about the telegraph office being a dead-end?" Evie asked when Tom drove right through the village.

"Are you trying to accuse me of having no faith in your abilities?" Tom asked in return.

Evie crossed her arms. "Well, as a matter of fact, I think I did rather well to discover the source of Miss Wainscot's rash." She had even surprised herself. She had no idea where she had learned to be so methodical or persistent.

"True," Tom said. "In fact, you did very well. I am impressed."

Evie grinned. "Why, thank you, kind sir. But why did you wait until now to tell me?"

"I'm sure I mentioned it."

Yes, he had. But his 'well done' remark had sounded almost absentminded.

When he stopped at the train station, Evie frowned at him. "What are we doing here?"

"How far do you think this roadster will get us? It's nearly two hundred miles to London."

London? "You're serious."

"You suggested it."

Yes, but she hadn't thought he would take her seriously. "We drove here, so I assumed... Oh, I don't know. How did we manage it?"

"In the larger car with extra canisters of gasoline and with a couple of suppliers along the way, that's how. And, let me tell you, this is not America. Those suppliers are few and far between. Anyhow, what did you think I was doing every time we stopped?"

Evie blushed. Every time they'd stopped, she'd actually closed her eyes because she'd thought Tom had needed to answer the call of nature...

Evie lifted her chin and looked ahead. "Never mind all that. If we don't hurry, we'll miss the train."

They strode the short distance, purchased their tickets and only had to wait a few minutes for the train to arrive.

As they were about to step into the First-Class compartment, Tom gave Evie an encouraging push.

"What's wrong?"

"Lady Penelope," Tom said. "She's boarding the same train. I guess she's serious about sorting out her wardrobe."

Evie peered out the window.

"She's in the next carriage." Tom checked his watch. "Why didn't she just telephone her dressmaker?"

"Perhaps because she'd like to organize someone else. Penelope is quite unforgiving. I've heard people refer to her as a quiet mouse who roars."

"Interesting," Tom mused.

"In what way?"

Shrugging, he said, "I wonder what triggers her sharp temperament."

Evie sat back and gave it some thought only to find herself thinking about Tom. He looked quite comfortable sitting opposite her.

If this had been the first time he'd traveled in first class, she would imagine he'd want to look around and see what he'd been missing out on. Come to think of it, he'd looked quite comfortable and confident when they'd visited Hainsley Hall.

There had been absolutely nothing to suggest he'd felt awkward.

Whenever she'd traveled to a new house with her maid, Caro, she'd noticed Caro looking around as if dazed by the sight of it all. Caro had almost grown up in large houses so she was used to it all. Even if the downstairs experience differed from that of the upstairs life, she was no stranger to the sight of a large house with all its extravagant furnishings and art works. And yet... she remained in awe of it all.

Not Tom.

"Have you thought about what I said earlier?" Tom asked.

"I'm afraid you'll have to remind me. I can't remember the last time I had to juggle so many thoughts at once. What with pretending I needed to run errands and looking for a dog I might or might not want and you bringing us to the station instead of stopping at the village... So, what else am I supposed to be thinking about?"

"What you might have in common with Bicky. We should still assume you are both targets. Why would someone want both of you out of the way? Who would stand to profit from that?"

Before she could compose a decent response, they were on their way. Evie looked out the window and watched the station disappear.

Tom cleared his throat. "I recall the Dowager Duchess saying you should have called her mama. Was there ever anything serious between you and the Duke?"

"The Dowager might have thought so... at the time.

I suppose it might have been an easy assumption to make. It's... It's a long story."

"And we have plenty of time."

Evie shifted. "Well... I suppose you could say I made a grand entrance. At the time, it would have been a big deal to have me as a house guest. Remember, I was a debutante."

He nodded. "I think what you mean to say is that you were an heiress. In other words, you were loaded."

"That too. Anyway, you've seen what it's like. When someone of note arrives at a large house, they usually organize quite a welcoming committee. From memory, the entire household had come out to greet me and they usually only do that for someone above an Earl or a Duke. Bicky had only recently become a Duke. Much had been expected of him and there I was, young, eligible and, as you pointed out, loaded." She'd been gracious and as polite as she could have been but the moment she had set eyes on Nicholas...

She'd been lost.

He hadn't been among the welcoming party. Evie remembered retiring to her room to change after her long journey. Caro had been sent up to help her dress and they'd formed an instant connection.

Frowning, Evie remembered Clara had attended that house party. Sitting up, she stared at Tom.

Clara had arrived the day before and, according to Caro, she had been instantly smitten by the young Earl of Woodridge. At the time, Evie had been overwhelmed by so many titles. She'd been a mere Miss, fresh off the boat, while all the other debutantes had hailed from the grandest houses in England.

Evie shook her head. "No, if Clara had meant to do anything, she would have taken action back then."

Tom smiled at her. "I think you need to fill me in on the rest. That sounded like the tail end of a conversation you had in your head."

"I suppose if I had to try and join the dots, I would say Clara resents me because I landed the man she wanted and the man she ended up with had been focused on winning me. Yes, Bicky had been interested."

Tom held her gaze for a long moment, and then he said, "I see."

"But it wouldn't make sense to wait all this time to do something about it."

"Wouldn't it? Back then, she might not have had the resources or the necessary female wiles to take action. Try to put yourself in her shoes. What would she do now that she couldn't do back then?"

Evie tipped her hat down to cover her eyes. She didn't want to think about this anymore. She couldn't. "Clara would have far too much to lose. She'd never risk landing in prison." But she could afford to pay someone else to do her bidding, Evie thought.

"Tell me about her. Is she the type to influence

people easily? Does she have an entourage of admirers? A lover? You've all hinted as much."

"Are you suggesting someone else might have done the deed for her?"

Tom shrugged. "It's possible."

Evie put on her best snooty tone and said, "Oh, darling. I have this pesky problem. It's really nothing but it would mean a great deal to me if someone were to take care of it for me."

"Precisely."

She couldn't. Could she?

CHAPTER 21

Hit and miss in bustling London

When they reached King's Cross Station, they stepped onto the platform and straight into a flurry of activity, but only after making sure Lady Penelope had already set off on her merry way to sort out her dressmaker problem.

"Now that we're here, where do we go?" Evie asked.

"The restaurant, of course. We could make discreet inquiries. Find out if the Duchess has been dining there. Is it far from here?"

Evie looked down at her shoes. She could manage a walk around the village, but anything more than that would be too strenuous. "We'll have to get a taxi."

As they strode out of the station, Evie took a moment to adjust to the different pace; the cars, the bicyclists and people… so many people hurrying by with such haste, they became a blur.

Evie wondered if Sergeant Newbury had unearthed anything of significance. As far as she knew, he had only interviewed Bicky's houseguests. She assumed he had also spoken with all the estate workers. If anyone new had been seen in the village, someone would have noticed.

The shooter had to be someone everyone knew.

Someone everyone trusted.

Evie wondered if the police had stepped up their investigation. After all, there had been an attempt on a peer's life…

During the drive to Piccadilly Circus, Evie talked about the dog she might get and avoided all mention of the subject uppermost in their minds for fear it would sound too odd to the driver.

"I hope you realize a dog will need to be walked a couple of times a day," Tom said.

Evie slanted her gaze toward him. "Yes, of course."

"And you'll also have to train him."

"You mean, teach him tricks?"

"To sit on command," he said.

"Oh, I suppose I could hire someone to do that for me."

"And where will it sleep?" he asked.

"I'm sure I could have something suitable made for him."

"A dog sized fourposter bed?"

Before she could answer, the taxi came to a stop outside the restaurant.

"I missed the sights," Evie said. "I should spend a day being a tourist." Seeing the customers walking into the restaurant, Evie tugged his sleeve. "I've just realized, we're not dressed properly."

"Pardon?"

"The clothes we're wearing. We're not dressed for lunch."

Tom pushed out a long breath. "We have traveled the length of England to get here and now you refuse to set foot inside a restaurant because you're wearing the wrong clothes. Would it be so bad if we walk in dressed as we are?"

Evie gave him a lifted eyebrow look. "We've come this far, let's not ruin it by making a bad impression or worse, being turned away."

While Evie turned to leave, Tom refused to budge.

"We're both foreigners," he said. "I'm sure they'll make an exception for us."

"Would you also like me to be loud, obnoxiously so? After all, it's almost excepted of Americans abroad."

The edge of his lip kicked up. "You sound offended."

"And I am." Evie's voice hitched. "Over the years,

I've had to endure so many prejudices, I don't wish to prove anyone right. I simply cannot do it. I won't."

A man striding by turned to look at Evie. A couple shook their heads.

Tom smiled. "See, you were just loud. I knew you had it in you."

When he took a step forward, Evie grabbed hold of his arm and dug her heels in.

"Are you honestly telling me you won't go inside because you're wearing the wrong dress?"

"I'm dressed for the country. This would be a major faux pas and… and it won't serve our purpose of blending in. I assume that's what we need to do."

Tom gave his jaw muscles a thorough workout. "What do you propose we do?"

"The house isn't far from here." She reached for his hand and checked his watch. "In fact, it will work out perfectly. We're far too early for lunch. That would make us even more obvious."

When they reached Evie's Mayfair house the butler, Edgar, barely batted an eyelash as he stepped aside to allow both the Countess of Woodridge and the chauffeur into the house.

While Evie had expected a different reaction from her stuffy butler, she felt too much relief to worry about it. In Evie's mind, another battle had been won as Tom had insisted going in through the servant's entrance.

Evie had put her foot down. "I really don't mean to stand outside my own home and argue with you. Now, do as you are told... Please."

The words rang in Evie's mind as she made her way up to her bedchamber with Edgar fast on her heels.

"My lady, Peters has taken the day off. Whom do you wish me to send up..."

"Edgar, please get a hold of yourself. I realize this is all out of the blue and I'm sorry for catching you unawares. If Millicent isn't here, then I shall have to manage by myself."

"B-by yourself, my lady?"

"Yes, Edgar. Now, please don't make a fuss. Mr. Winchester and I will show ourselves out. No need to stand on ceremony."

Evie thought she heard Edgar murmur Tom's name under his breath as if in disbelief. A sure sign he had noticed Tom's entrance by the front door. When he emitted a huff, Evie stopped and turned.

"Edgar. You are beyond reproach. Your service to me has been exemplary."

He bowed his head.

"If you have anything to say, anything appropriate to say, then do so within my hearing. Otherwise... Well, I really must get on."

"As you wish, my lady."

"I do wish it, Edgar."

Evie went through her wardrobe and wondered how Caro or Millicent managed to make such swift selections from so many choices. It seemed for every choice she made, she had to make two more.

She settled on a pale green dress and matched it with the softest shade of fawn shoes with double straps only because she found a hat with both colors on it.

When she finished dressing, she checked the clock on the mantle and realized it had taken her an entire hour to change.

Caro and Millicent definitely earned their keep and deserved a raise.

As she strode down the stairs, she suddenly realized Tom wouldn't have anything suitable to wear since all the clothes he had been producing had come from the man he'd met at the pub, Sir Bradford.

Belatedly, she realized that had probably been the reason why he'd tried to talk her into going into the restaurant dressed as they had been. He'd known he wouldn't have anything appropriate to change into.

By the time she reached the bottom of the stairs, she had given herself a good talking to. "So help me, I will never again assume…"

Edgar cleared his throat.

Evie looked around the entrance hall and saw no sign of Tom.

"What have you done with Tom?"

Her butler's eyebrows shot up. "I'm not sure I know what you mean, my lady."

"Tom Winchester. I expected him to be waiting for me here."

"Mr. Winchester is waiting for your ladyship outside."

Mr. Winchester?

There hadn't been an ounce of mockery in Edgar's tone. In fact, he'd used the reverence reserved for royalty.

Holding the front door open for Evie, Edgar inclined his head.

Evie took a step forward only to stop. "Mr. Winchester?"

"Yes, my lady."

"Tom Winchester."

"One and the same, my lady."

"And you don't have a problem with that?"

"I don't believe I do, my lady."

Something had transpired, but she didn't have any time to delve. "Please don't alert the staff of my arrival. In fact, pretend as if I'm not here."

"As you wish, my lady."

Evie strode out almost in a daze. If she didn't know better, she'd think Edgar had been bribed into compliance.

Lost in her thoughts, she experienced the second

surprise of the day. Although, if she really thought about it, her entire day had been filled with them.

She found Tom leaning against a roadster. He had swapped his country tweed suit for a smart ensemble of the finest cut. The light gray suit, white shirt and sea green tie, matched with caramel brown brogues, complimented her clothes.

"I suppose I should apologize for taking so long," Evie said in her breeziest tone, "but you might not have noticed my tardiness since you were probably busy mugging someone for their clothes."

Smiling, he held the car door open for her.

Evie wanted to say something about the motor car, but she couldn't get her mind off the fact he had managed to procure an entire outfit from thin air while she had battled through an already available selection.

As she settled into the passenger seat, she said, "I suppose I should ask where your clothes and the car came from, but then I would also have to ask about Edgar. I'm sure you did something to him and he'll never be the same again."

Tom smiled. "The less you know, the better."

"I paid good money to get a stuffy butler of the first order. I hope you haven't damaged him." She looked around her. "This car smells new." And his clothes looked new.

Sitting back, she decided to leave it all alone. Her

resolution lasted two seconds. Leaning toward him, she sniffed him.

That earned her a raised eyebrow look.

"You look and smell cleanshaven."

As he took off, his sleeve shifted enough to reveal his watch. It looked different to the one he'd worn earlier.

Again, Evie leaned in and, tugging his sleeve back, she had a closer look.

"We have plenty of time," he said.

Time... courtesy of the oldest luxury watch manufacturing company, Patek Philippe.

Evie had a horde of questions but she kept them to herself and settled for watching Tom expertly weave his way through London traffic.

"People seem to be growing attached to their motor cars," she remarked. They had already converted the stables at the house into a place to house the motor car. She had the room for it, but not everyone did. "I almost yearn for the days of horse drawn carriages..." In the next breath, she said, "I think I should have called the restaurant and made a booking for us."

"No need to worry. It's been taken care of."

Evie slanted her gaze toward him, her curiosity urging her to ask for clarification. "With so much taken care of, I hope the Duchess complies and makes this impromptu trip to London worth our while. It would be unkind of her to ruin our haphazard plans by not turning up."

"And if she had a generous bone in her body," he said, "she could even own up to plotting both your downfall and Bicky's?"

"Yes, that would be perfectly lovely of her. Of course, I would then have to pay her a visit in prison…"

CHAPTER 22

Rumor has it...

The Criterion, Piccadilly Circus

They sat at a central table with an uninterrupted view of the famous Criterion Long Bar with its marble and blue and white ornamentation and glistening ceiling of gold mosaic. When the waiter presented the lamb dish, Evie tried to recall how they'd made their way to a main course. She knew they'd placed an order but their attention had been fixed on the still absent Duchess.

Evie even struggled to remember why they had come chasing after her.

Soon after arriving, Evie had insisted on cutting to the chase and establishing whether or not the Duchess had been lunching at the Criterion.

The Maître d' had been quite accommodating but only after Tom had slipped him a bill.

Yes, Her Grace had recently become a regular diner.

Would she be here today?

Yes, they certainly hoped to be graced by her presence.

And yet...

Her Grace had yet to make an appearance.

Before the waiter moved away, Evie asked, "Has the Duchess of Hetherington already lunched today?"

"No, my lady. We're expecting her soon."

When the waiter strode away, Tom smiled. "Patience doesn't seem to be one of your virtues."

"No, not today. The Duchess is either a significant piece of the puzzle or a not so innocent bystander." Evie wished they'd been able to establish her intentions. If only they'd found a letter hinting at her dissatisfaction with her marriage and her plans to do everything in her power to dissolve it.

"She's flaunting her affair right under his nose by her very absence," Evie muttered. If Bicky wanted to part ways, he would need solid evidence of adultery and he would have it with ease. But Evie knew he would never travel down that path. "She thinks she's above it all."

"We don't have proof yet," Tom said.

Disregarding him, Evie added, "With such an uncooperative husband, she might resort to force and something more final." Arranging a small portion of food onto her fork, Evie tried to savor it, but her heart simply wouldn't oblige her with the enthusiasm required.

"You must be pleased," she said, "after all, we're here at your insistence. I hope you're not expecting to get your way with my dog. Be warned, I will choose the one I want."

Tom reached for his glass of champagne and lifted it as if about to toast her. "So, you've decided which breed you want."

Evie's chin rose slightly. "Maybe." She looked around and then set her mind to rearranging the food on her plate.

Tom sighed. "She will come."

"How can you be so sure? The Maître d' might have been using her as a piece of publicity. Yes, Her Grace is one of our grandest patrons. He probably employs a stooge to murmur in prospective diners' ears, enticing them to the establishment with promises of rubbing shoulders with a Duchess."

"As a matter of fact, I phoned ahead," Tom revealed.

"What? When?"

"Before we left the house."

"Which house? Mine?"

"No, Bicky's."

"You knew all along we would encounter the Duchess here and that's why you insisted we trek all the way down to London and you didn't tell me?"

"Well, the alternative would have been to pursue another lead and force the post mistress' hand. I believe I made my feelings on the matter quite clear. Although, in hindsight, I'm sure you would have found a way to extricate the information without appearing to break any rules."

"Where there's a will... And yes, I'm still puzzling over Penelope's behavior." And she still believed there might have been something of interest in that telegram. "She always makes such a fuss when she doesn't get her way. You wouldn't know it by her quiet demeanor, but she can be a hard task master. I pity her lady's maid. Caro tells me she lives in fear of being fired with no letter of reference. You really wouldn't know it by the way she behaves in the drawing room."

"Since you're obsessing about her, what do you think she could be capable of and why?" Tom asked.

"Any number of things. The fact she can juggle such contrasting characters makes her rather enigmatic and untrustworthy. I've never really thought about it before, but now she's given me reason to further analyze her behavior."

"And so, we can expect anything from her."

"Precisely." Evie waited for Tom to ask about her motive for taking any sort of action against her or Bicky but his attention shifted. And just as well because she wouldn't have been able to come up with a motive even if her life depended on it. Which it did...

Turning slightly, Evie gasped. "There she is." She swung back around and lowered her head.

"Don't you want her to see you?" Tom asked.

Evie reached for her glass of champagne and gulped it down. Never in a million years would she have guessed...

"She's sitting down two tables away from us," Tom said.

"The man she's with," Evie managed to say before a waiter appeared and refilled her glass. "He's married," Evie whispered.

"So is she."

"Yes, but... He is married to Penelope." Had the telegram contained information about his affair?

"Lady Penelope?"

"Yes."

Tom chuckled. "I know I've only known you for a couple of months, but I don't believe I've ever seen you so wound up."

"I feel we are being diverted, led on a merry dance in order to confuse us or take our minds off what really matters. Don't you think it's strange how we haven't even been able to establish who the real target is?"

"You might have a point." Tom quirked his eyebrow up. "They're being very amorous. If they're carrying on an illicit affair, shouldn't they try to be more discreet?"

Perhaps not, Evie thought.

"What are you thinking?" Tom asked.

"This might be their way of forcing their spouses' hands." She knew Bicky would never agree to a divorce. Nor would Penelope. As heir to his father's title, Lord Hammond was in line to provide Penelope with the much-coveted title of Countess, something she would not give up easily. "Remember when Bicky spoke about his growing cynicism?"

Tom nodded. "Matthew spoke against it, saying neither he nor his wife were in any hurry to take over the responsibilities associated with the title."

Evie huffed. "The same can't be said for Penelope." As a debutante, she'd been a wallflower. From what Evie had heard, her marriage to Lord Hammond had been quite a coup, brought about by the fact Penelope's father had been able to provide a substantial dowry. "Her marriage and her status did not come easily to her. I can assure you, she will not be pleased about any of this."

Lord Hammond would survive a divorce, especially if steps had been taken to tie up Penelope's dowry. Regardless, if he planned on pursuing more than a liaison with the Duchess of Hetherington, he would benefit from her vast fortune. Her marriage contract must have been costly, but her family had done very well out of their coal findings.

Evie gasped. "Bicky will never agree to a divorce."

"Meaning?"

"In order to be free to marry the Duchess, Lord Hammond would need to get Bicky out of the way."

"And you think he would take drastic steps to achieve his goal?" Tom asked.

"He probably thinks being in London gives him the perfect alibi."

Frowning, Tom said, "Where do you fit into the picture?"

Good question. "I... I could be the smokescreen, used to divert attention from his master plan." She tilted her head in thought and played around with the idea of Lord Hammond as the mastermind. "Are they still carrying on?"

Tom nodded. "See for yourself."

"I don't dare. The sight of them together might keep me awake at night or I might be tempted into giving them a piece of my mind and that would surely cause a scene."

"That's odd," Tom murmured.

"Are you taunting me? I told you, I refuse to look."

"Well, he keeps looking over his shoulder toward

the entrance. If I had to guess, I'd say he's expecting someone."

Evie cupped her hands around her eyes.

Tom laughed. "Did you just put your blinkers on?"

"I'm thinking. What if Lord Hammond sent Penelope a telegram saying he would be here with the Duchess as a challenge for her to do something or accept her fate?"

Tom sat back and brushed his hand across his chin. "That's an interesting theory. He might have sent it anonymously and since Penelope didn't show anyone the telegram, only she knows the contents."

"Meaning?" She didn't wait for Tom to answer. "This would be her perfect opportunity to strike." She had no trouble seeing Penelope in a new light. After receiving the challenge from her cheating husband, she would have put a plan into motion, creating an alibi for herself by saying she needed to rush down to London and sort out her wardrobe problems. "Would she do it herself or organize someone else to do the deed?" And what would she do?

"Are you now thinking Penelope will take her revenge and kill or have her husband killed?"

Evie nodded.

"But wouldn't that defeat the purpose? She would then be without a husband and a title."

True. "Unless…"

Tom leaned in. "Unless?"

"She might have someone else lined up."

A wave of murmurs swept through the restaurant. Tom straightened and gazed around. Then, nudging his head toward the entrance, he said, "Ah, I see what he's been waiting for."

The flash of a photograph being taken had everyone gasping.

"If the commotion is anything to go by, I suspect there might be more than one secret rendezvous taking place here," Evie mused. "I'll also have to agree with you. This is what Lord Hammond has been waiting for." Had he set himself and the Duchess up so they could have photographic proof to show their respective spouses?

CHAPTER 23

Another wardrobe change...

"*L*et me guess, we cannot possibly travel in these clothes," Tom said under his breath in response to Evie's insistence they drive back to the Mayfair house.

When they arrived, Evie assured him, "It shouldn't take as long this time. I'll only be changing back into my traveling clothes. In any case, if we're to make it back in time for dinner we should hurry and catch the next train." As she strode into the house, she asked, "What will you do about your new motor car?"

"Edgar can take care of it."

Could he, indeed? Striding up the stairs, Evie

wondered what had been going on right under her nose. The thought kept her mind engaged throughout the half hour it took her to change into her traveling clothes.

"You're very quiet," Tom remarked as they made their way to the train station in a taxi.

"Oh, yes… I've been wondering about the stables we had converted for the motor car."

"What about it?"

"Well, I wonder how many cars I would find there. You see, I've never set foot inside the stables." For all she knew, Tom might be keeping a collection of cars and clothes for every occasion.

"King's Cross Station," the taxi driver announced.

Evie took care of the payment and Tom held the door open for her. She stepped out and looked up only to gasp. Grabbing hold of Tom's sleeve, she said to the taxi driver, "One moment, please."

She shoved Tom back inside the taxi and said, "Driver, follow that car."

Tom looked around him and asked, "What? Who?"

Still holding on to his sleeve, Evie said, "I just saw Penelope emerging from a car." With her free hand, she pointed ahead. "That one there."

"We'll miss our train," Tom said under his breath.

"Never mind that."

"What do you base your hasty decision on?" Tom whispered.

"Penelope supposedly came to town to sort out her wardrobe. Yet, here she was being dropped off in a private car."

Frowning, Tom asked, "Wouldn't it have been easier to approach her on the train and ask her?"

"Oh, I suppose so." Grinning, Evie added, "But this is more fun." She tapped the front seat. "Driver, it's making a turn. Don't let it get away."

"Anyone would think you're reluctant to return to Yarborough," Tom mused. "Are you afraid of upsetting Bicky with the bad news?"

"He can't be upset by something he already knows. I suspect Penelope has also been made aware of the situation. Don't worry, we'll catch the next train. That car appears to be headed toward..." She looked around. "Driver, where are we now?"

"Knightsbridge."

Evie tapped the driver's seat again. "It's slowing down. Now it's turning."

The taxi driver followed at a discreet distance. "You seem to have done this before," Evie remarked.

"I've had some strange requests," he agreed. He brought the taxi to a stop and pointed at the side of a house. "It's going in there, into the carriage house. What would you like me to do?"

Evie sat back. They needed to find out who lived in that house attached to the carriage house.

Sighing, Tom eased the door open. "The chauffeur is coming out to have a cigarette. I'll go see if I can engage him in conversation."

Evie watched him cross the street and approach the driver. "When he returns," Evie told the driver, "drive half way down the street so the chauffeur doesn't see him climbing into the taxi."

Evie had never been a nail biter. Yet, she found herself nibbling the tip of her finger. The area of Knightsbridge remained exclusive to those who could afford to live there. It stood to reason, the owner would have to be someone of note.

Seeing Tom striding away from the chauffeur, Evie tapped the taxi driver on the shoulder. "You can move along a bit, just enough so the chauffeur doesn't see us." They wouldn't want to make him suspicious in case he mentioned something to his employer...

When Tom climbed in, the taxi driver turned, his eyes brightening with interest.

"Drive on, please," Evie said. "We need to head back to King's Cross Station." And she would have to practice some patience.

Evie fiddled with her small handbag. She opened it and closed it several times. Finally, she drew out a small book.

Out of the corner of her eye, she saw Tom leaning in and trying to read the title on the cover.

"It's a new book… by a new author." She showed him the cover. "F. Scott Fitzgerald. I picked it up before we left New York." She settled down to read. Ten minutes later, she remained on the same page. Her eyes drifted to the top of the page. She must have read the name Amory Blaine a dozen times and each time she forgot she'd read it and every time she read it, she whispered, "Who is Amory Blaine?"

Finally, the taxi stopped outside the station.

"I'll check the times for the next train," Tom said, sounding almost relieved as he hurried on ahead.

Evie followed him at a sedate pace and met him at the station entrance.

"We're in luck. We only have ten minutes to wait until the next train."

"Meanwhile, you can tell me what you found out from the chauffeur." She watched him chew the inside of his lip. Evie tilted her head. "Tom, does my small talk bother you?"

He shoved his hands inside his pockets. "Not exactly."

"So, it does… somewhat."

"I wouldn't go so far as to say that."

"Would you say you find it annoying?"

"No. It's… quaint. But, since you mention it, when you whisper something, do you actually require a response? Because, if you do, I have no idea who Amory Blaine is."

"Oh, that... No, I don't require a response." Evie perked up. "Now, can you tell me what you found out from the chauffeur?"

Tom raked his fingers through his hair.

"Yes, I feel I should apologize. Sometimes, my mind wanders and... Well, I do go off topic a bit. I wonder if I picked the trait up from Charlotte?" Seeing him frowning, she smiled. "I did it again. Please continue."

"Alexander Fleshling."

Evie gasped. "No! Bicky's heir?"

"Yes. It's his London house."

"What could Penelope have been doing there?" she asked as they reached the platform. Half an hour later, as the train rocked and started on its journey, Evie still hadn't managed to answer the question. "I fear the worst," Evie said.

"And what might that be?" Tom asked.

"I always try to see the best side of people, but in order to make sense of this situation, I might have to abandon the practice and start thinking the worst."

The Great War had shaken everyone's lives and opened their eyes to the grimmer side of life, but somehow, people had found a way to move on.

Evie liked to think she had been lost in the darkness and now she had found her way to the light again. However, the events of the last couple of days had awoken something inside her. Suddenly, she under-stood Bicky's cynicism.

"Someone is being motivated by self-interest," Evie murmured. "When I first told Bicky about the incident on the road, he asked who stood to inherit. I've been so side-tracked I forgot to check up on my young charge." Then again, he was surrounded by family retainers; with some claiming several generations of faithful service.

"Seth Halton?"

"Yes." Evie held up her hand. "Before you jump to conclusions, I am once again being side-tracked. At the time, I wondered if someone new had come into Seth's life, someone who might be trying to influence him."

"Isn't Seth Halton only seven years old?" Tom asked.

"Yes, and I feel guilty. I should be showing a greater interest in him." She supposed Elizabeth hadn't been the only one to go into deep mourning. Tilting her head, she added, "You are clearly well informed. Is there anything you don't know about me?" Once again, her hand went up. "No, don't answer that. It might make life awkward between us."

The edge of Tom's lip kicked up. "You were saying…?"

"Oh, yes. Self-interest. Bicky has been on the right track all along. Who stands to benefit? That's what we should have been asking all along, but the answer might not be as obvious as it seems."

"If I had to guess, I'd say Penelope, Lady Hammond, stands to benefit the most."

"Yes, I'd have to agree."

His jaw muscle twitched. "I took a wild stab but you sound quite sure. Care to share your thoughts?"

"Give me a moment. I need to think about the ideas taking shape in my mind." Evie closed her eyes…

"Evie."

Her eyes fluttered open and she scrambled to sit up. "I didn't. Please tell me I didn't fall asleep."

"You closed your eyes," Tom said. "About an hour ago. At first, I didn't wish to interrupt your thinking process, but then it became obvious you had fallen asleep and it would have been too cruel to wake you up."

Evie straightened. "Oh, I beg your pardon. I guess all the excitement tired me out." She looked out the window.

"We're nearly there," he said.

Evie's eyes widened. She pressed her hands to her cheeks. "Oh, no. It's gone. I had a thought." She tapped her forehead. "It came to me and then I woke up and… Now it's gone."

"Don't worry. It will come to you."

She sat back and tried to tease her mind into

revealing the thoughts that had surged to the surface. "This has nothing to do with what I'm trying to remember."

"Go on."

"Well, in case I forget, as I'm sure I will. Would you please remind me to check on Seth Halton? He is in safe hands, but it wouldn't hurt to check. We need to pay him a visit and see how he is getting on. I receive regular reports but when Bicky asked who stood to inherit, I couldn't help wondering if someone new had come into Seth's life."

"Yes, you mentioned that before you trailed off and fell asleep. So, you think someone new has come into his life and might be trying to influence him?" Tom asked.

"Yes, perhaps I should consider spending more time at Woodridge House." At some point, she would need to realize no amount of time would suffice to make her memories fade.

She felt the train slowing down and saw the station appear. At one end, the station master kept a watchful eye on the platform. Porters hurried about. A chauffeur stood at attention. The times she had traveled to Yarborough by train, she had been met at the station by a Yarborough Manor chauffeur and she'd also had Caro to organize everything for her. Her arrival had always been filled with excitement at the prospect of seeing a friendly face. Now...

"I have the strangest feeling. Almost like the calm before the storm," she murmured.

To Evie's surprise, they drove back to Yarborough Manor in silence. However, as they drove through the village, Evie remembered Penelope's telegram. Would they have discovered anything worth their while?

"Alexander Fleshling must have sent the telegram," she mused.

"Are you about to suggest we sneak into Lady Hammond's bedchamber to look for it?"

"Not we. One of us, but not both of us. Someone should make sure she doesn't go upstairs while the other one searches her room."

"If he did send the telegram," Tom said, "I doubt he will have used his real name. Even if we manage to connect her to Alexander, what will that prove?"

"Collusion," Evie declared. "They're in on something... together." She would have to speak with Bicky and tackle the difficult subject of his wife. If Clara had asked him for a divorce, he might have refused...

Evie shook her head. Clara would most definitely have asked for a divorce and he would most certainly have refused and that might have driven Clara to take drastic steps.

Tom cleared his throat. "Earlier, you felt sure Penelope wouldn't risk anything getting in the way of the title. She must know her husband is having an affair and yet she chooses to turn a blind eye to it."

"I was just playing around with the idea of Clara pushing for a divorce and taking matters into her own hands." Evie tapped her chin in thought. "Yes, and that's why she's having an affair with Lord Hammond. They are both determined and have decided to kill two birds with one affair."

Tom turned his focus to the winding road but Evie could sense him tossing the ideas around. When the road straightened, he said, "What would you do in Lady Hammond's place?"

Evie's unladylike snort made her laugh. "My apologies. I just entertained two images in my mind and one of them involved tar and feathers. If I had to wear Penelope's shoes... I would definitely not lower myself to my spouse's despicable level."

"So, you would maintain your moral high ground."

"Absolutely. My reputation would need to remain above reproach. It's a woman's lot in life but a necessary one. We always seem to be held to higher accountability."

"It doesn't seem to be bothering the Duchess."

"You have no idea how much I am struggling to understand her reasoning. She would have, if not killed, then maimed someone in order to win the coveted title. Why would she throw it all away now?"

"Are you thinking out loud or do you wish to hear my opinion?" Tom asked.

"If you have something to share, by all means, share it."

"As I've said before, I am still a wildcatter at heart. The Duchess would put everything on the line only if she had more to gain."

"More of what?"

"Money."

CHAPTER 24

Her kingdom for a horse

Yarborough Manor

"Sage green?" Caro asked.

Evie gave her a distracted nod. They'd arrived in time for a late afternoon tea but Evie had been too tired to join in so she'd retired to her room for a rest. If Tom had heard any worthwhile news, he had clearly chosen to wait until Evie went down to tell her.

"Did you enjoy your day out, milady?"

Evie nodded. "Yes, but it wore me out." Straightening, Evie asked, "Is Lady Hammond's maid any better at conversing with the other staff members these days. I know you've said she tends to keep to herself, but I wonder if you've worked your charm on her."

"I've tried but Miss Shard is even quieter than usual."

"Do you think you might try again? I get the feeling Lady Hammond's marriage is facing difficult times. If that's the case, I'd like to tread with care." Or rather, she'd like to have solid confirmation. An affair did not necessarily signal the end of a marriage.

"More marital problems… There must be some sort of epidemic going around," Caro murmured.

"Will you ask?"

"Yes, milady. I shouldn't have any trouble finding Miss Shard."

"Oh, you sound sure."

Caro nodded. "She has spent the afternoon in the kitchen doing some mending. Soon after arriving from the station, Lady Hammond dismissed Miss Shard and took to her bed complaining of a headache."

"Oh, I hope Lady Penelope feels well enough to join us."

"I'm not sure she will. Her headache appears to be quite severe."

Evie stared at her reflection. Had Penelope discovered something upsetting during her visit to London?

Perhaps she had only suspected her husband had been having an affair and she finally had confirmation of it.

What if Alexander Fleshling had put her onto her husband's affair? More and more, Evie suspected the telegram had been from him. For all she knew, Penelope might have made her way to the Criterion and seen her husband with the Duchess with her own eyes. But why would Alexander Fleshling involve her?

"Is something wrong, milady?"

"Why do you ask?"

Caro signaled to the wedge between Evie's eyebrows and, smiling, she said, "If the wind changes, you will remain like that forever."

"I wonder... Could you go and see how Lady Hammond is faring? You can say I'm concerned about her. And, while you're at it, could you look around her room for a piece of paper? Well, not exactly a piece of paper. A telegram, to be exact."

Moments later, Evie strode down the stairs. Half way down, she stopped and, looking up, she wondered if perhaps she should look in on Penelope.

It couldn't be easy on her.

Penelope's behavior had always been beyond reproach. She would, no doubt, see her husband's affair as reflecting badly on her. It wouldn't hurt to offer assurances...

Then again, she might not welcome the intrusion. Poor woman, Evie thought and thanked her lucky stars she had found a decent man who'd only had eyes for her.

Thinking Penelope would most likely prefer to be left alone, Evie strode down to the drawing room. After exchanging a few pleasantries with the other guests, she went to sit next to Bicky.

"Was your trip fruitful?" he asked. "Tom mentioned you'd gone to London."

She glanced over at Tom but he was deep in conversation with Mark Harper, Viscount Maison and Lady Gloriana.

"Did Tom say anything else?" Evie asked.

"No, he left that up to you, which I found rather enigmatic. Then I realized the subject needed to be tackled by you because it required some delicacy. I hope I'm wrong."

Evie took a deep swallow. "W-we followed a hunch and went to the Criterion." She held his gaze for a moment as she tried to gather her courage. "I'm so sorry, Bicky."

His smile faltered. "You saw Clara."

"Yes." She placed her hand on his.

He nodded. "I take it she wasn't alone."

Evie gave a slow shake of her head. "Has she spoken to you about…"

"Divorce?" Bicky laughed. "It's been her favorite topic of conversation for over a year now."

Lowering her voice, she asked, "Is it worth holding on?" Her gaze dropped to his arm.

"You think she had something to do with this."

Evie couldn't help but admire the calm resignation in his voice. "I suspect she might be in collusion with..." She drew in a breath and wished she'd rehearsed what she had to say to him. "We saw her with Hammond." Lord Hammond, Viscount Hammond, heir to the Earl of Remington. How could he do this to Penelope? The scandal would follow him until the end of days.

To her surprise, Bicky didn't bat an eyelash.

"Did you know?" she asked.

"She made a point of telling me." He stole a furtive glance across the room. "Penelope is in denial. I've tried to speak to her about it but she won't hear a bad word said against her husband."

Evie supposed Penelope had far too much to lose. "Frankly, I'm surprised. You know what she's like when things don't go her way. I would have expected her to make a fuss."

"As strange as it might sound, I'm sorry for Hammond," Bicky said. "I'm afraid Clara has sunk her claws into him only because she needs someone to help her drive the message home. Of course, she couldn't carry on with anyone lower than a soon to be Earl."

"Doesn't she realize what it will cost her?"

"Not her fortune," Bicky said. "The dowry is all tied

up but her uncle died without issue and left her everything. That's when she made up her mind to ask for a divorce."

"It must be a veritable fortune for her to walk away from all this," Evie remarked.

"It is. Back in the 1850s, her uncle took his Grand Tour money and set himself up as a pastoralist in Australia. He thought he'd make his fortune in sheep. Would you believe it? He struck gold right on his property."

"I'm guessing he found more than a few nuggets."

Bicky snorted. "I've tried to put it into perspective. He did very well indeed with one of the biggest gold finds in the area. In fact, everyone seems to have done well out of the venture. Did you know, the gold exported to Britain from Australia in the 1850s paid all her foreign debts?"

"Golly!" Regardless, Evie couldn't quite understand how Clara would face the consequences of a divorce. Especially within their circle, Evie thought. Everyone had moved with the times, facing a great many changes which appeared to crop up at a rate of knots, but most people still disapproved.

"Drink?" Bicky offered as he accepted a glass from Larkin.

"No, thank you. I should keep a clear head." She waited for Larkin to move away before saying, "I've been wondering if Clara would try something..."

Bicky laughed. "You mean, try to kill me?"

"Well, yes. But now I'm not so sure. Until now, I thought she only had her social standing to worry about losing, but now you say there's a vast fortune involved. She wouldn't want to risk losing that."

"I suppose money does corrupt." He raised his glass and gestured toward Tom. "It doesn't seem to have affected Tom Winchester."

"What do you mean?"

"Well, he's gone from nothing to everything and yet it didn't stop him from volunteering in the war."

It hadn't stopped Bicky either. "Yes, I suppose he doesn't mind getting his hands dirty." Evie glanced at Tom and silently congratulated him on a job well done. He certainly had done well, selling everyone a credible story about himself.

"Bicky, as a friend, I feel I should urge you to consider walking away. Let her go. She can't be worth the trouble."

Bicky looked over her shoulder and said, "I believe your maid is trying to attract your attention."

Turning, Evie saw Caro peering at her from the doorway. "Excuse me, please." She rushed toward her. "Did you find something?"

"Yes, milady. Miss Shard was busy in the kitchen mending. She looked quite upset but she wouldn't tell me why. Anyhow, I took the opportunity to go into Lady Penelope's bedchamber. I died a thousand deaths when I saw her lying on the bed, but when she didn't stir, I took a chance to look around." She dug inside her pocket and produced a piece of paper. "I found this on her dresser."

"Thank you, Caro. You're a treasure." Taking the note, Evie returned to sit beside Bicky and read the telegram. "Noon. Today. Glad you changed your mind." Evie looked up. "It's not signed."

"A message from your secret admirer?" Bicky asked.

Evie explained her suspicions about the telegram Penelope had received earlier and how she and Tom had seen Penelope being dropped off at the train station and had then followed the motor car to Knightsbridge. She watched for Bicky's response. When he stopped blinking, she knew he'd made a connection of sorts.

Evie took a deep swallow and wished she didn't have to be the bearer of such ill tidings. "Alexander Fleshling's chauffeur drove Penelope to the train station. She'd been to see Alexander," Evie said.

"Funny, she never mentioned anything, but then... why would she?"

"Oh? When did you see Penelope?"

"She came down earlier on. I was in here waiting for everyone to come in." He looked across at the piano. "I'd been playing a tune. Larkin had just set a cup of coffee down and... Oh, I forgot to drink it. Anyhow, she talked about her dressmaker and what a disappointment she'd been. A moment later, she excused herself and said she needed to take a powder for her headache. I hope she's all right. She must be in a bad way. I couldn't help feeling she looked a little lost and confused."

"My maid just went up and she said Penelope is sleeping." Evie folded the piece of paper and lifted her eyes. "Bicky. When was the last time you saw Alexander?"

Bicky took a sip of his drink. "Let me think. He came for Christmas and before that, he came over for the grouse season. Said he needed to get in more practice, just in case." Bicky laughed. "He's always joking about that because we're the same age and... Well, what are the chances I'll go before he does."

"So, he's not likely to inherit. Is that what he thinks?"

Bicky finished his drink. "I've been trying to encourage him to settle down and produce an heir. As it is, I doubt I will. Certainly not under my current circumstances."

"And how does he feel about that?"

Bicky pressed his glass to his lips and took a quick drink. "Are you suggesting he might be somehow involved in some sordid plan to get rid of me?"

"If I say yes, I'm afraid I would then struggle to explain why someone took a shot at me."

Bicky gestured to Larkin who promptly produced a

refill. Surging to his feet, he steadied himself and then strode over to the window.

Evie followed.

Glancing at her, he gave her a brisk smile. "My apologies. The thought of Alexander being in any way involved in something as macabre as... No, I can't even bring myself to say it."

"What would happen if you granted Clara her divorce?" Evie asked.

"You know it is my duty to marry again."

They stared at each other, neither one speaking or even blinking, but both clearly doing a great deal of thinking.

If Bicky fathered an heir, Alexander Fleshling would be out of the running. Surely, he must have known all along that would happen. For as long as Bicky lived, Alexander could only be a placeholder. His position would always be tenuous as Bicky was bound to father an heir...

Evie wondered about his financial situation. He had to be doing well enough to be able to afford a house in Knightsbridge. Nevertheless, she asked, "What does he do?"

"He's in banking. Does quite well for himself."

Yes, but for some people doing well didn't seem to be enough. For others, having all the money in the world wouldn't be enough...

His wife wanted a divorce. His current heir... no

doubt, wanted to secure his position. The only person standing in the way of it all seemed to be reluctant to face reality.

"Bicky, when did Clara leave for London?"

"A week ago."

Evie struggled to picture spending an entire week trying on clothes. Then, another thought struck. She'd sent Bicky a message just over a week ago. "Out of curiosity, did you happen to keep my letter saying I would be attending your house party?"

"Of course, I keep everything. I mean…" He cast his eye around the room. "Everyone in my family keeps everything. I can tell you what my great grandfather ate for lunch all those years ago."

Evie nibbled the edge of her lip. Finally, she said, "All along, I've been saying you were the only one who knew of my arrival."

He nodded.

"Do you think Clara read the letter?"

His face paled. He managed to whisper, "She might have…" Raking his fingers through his hair, he swung away.

Evie wondered if they were entertaining the same thoughts. Clara might have organized someone to take a shot at Bicky. Years' worth of resentment might have made Evie a target too. Or, as she'd thought earlier, a convenient ruse. A smokescreen to divert everyone's attention away from the real target.

Bicky looked up at the ceiling. "I suppose with me out of the way, she would have gained her freedom without the inconvenience of a scandalous divorce."

"What will you do?" Evie asked.

"If I confront her, she'll only deny it. We have no proof of wrongdoing."

He would need proof of his wife's plot. If Clara had hired someone, there might be a money trail.

And then... there was Alexander.

He might be behind all this. It would just be a matter of discovering what role he'd played.

Larkin cleared his throat and approached Tom. "Mr. Winchester. There is a telephone call for you."

Evie watched him leave. She wished she'd thought of including him in the conversation. Now, she would have to remember everything she'd discussed with Bicky.

When Tom returned, he looked straight at Evie, his expression serious enough for Evie to wonder if she'd have to offer an apology for something she wasn't even aware she'd said or done.

Tom hadn't even reached her when Larkin cleared his throat again and announced, "Her Grace, The Dowager Duchess of Heatherington."

The Dowager stopped at the threshold. Looking around the drawing room, she smiled and nodded and then she met Charlotte's gaze. "Ah, there you are, Lady Charlotte."

Tom sidled up to Evie. "Should we lineup and wait our turn? She appears to be on the warpath."

Evie forced herself to chuckle, all the while thinking about poor Bicky. "You can consider yourself safe if she smiled at you. Although, her smile can be deceiving."

The Duchess strode up to Charlotte and said, "I have a few choice words to impart to you, my dear."

Charlotte must have been caught unawares because she actually brightened. "Oh, do tell."

"Word about your insinuations and accusations disrupted my afternoon tea. I am told you hold me entirely responsible for my son's close encounter with death because, in your opinion, I have finally cracked it." The Dowager's voice hitched. "Yes, indeed. Cracked it."

Evie glanced at the footmen standing at attention. They had been the only ones to hear Charlotte. Had they taken the news down to the kitchen?

Tom cupped Evie's elbow and guided her to the window. Lowering his voice, he said, "I received a phone call from the Sergeant. He wishes us to call in at the police station tomorrow morning."

"Us? Why?"

"They have apprehended a suspect."

CHAPTER 25

Bon appetite

"$\mathcal{M}$r. Winchester. Is there something you wish to share with the rest of us?" the Dowager demanded.

"I feel like a naughty schoolboy being reprimanded," Tom whispered. "My apologies, Duchess. It seems there has been a new development in the investigation. The authorities might have found the shooter."

"Oh, I see. So, they're still not certain. We should perhaps focus on what we do know. Facts, my dear boy. Charlotte thinks I have finally cracked it and I would like everyone to do their part and dissuade her from such a delusion."

Everyone turned their attention to Charlotte who had shrunk back into her chair.

"It seems the Dowager can dish it out but she can't take it," Tom whispered.

"I'm sure she'll keep it short, otherwise she would have come earlier. Although… Maybe she's gearing herself up to take over the dinner conversation."

The butler cleared his throat.

"I suppose that's dinner, Larkin." Bicky swept his gaze around the drawing room. "Shall we?"

The exodus left the Dowager flabbergasted. "But I haven't finished yet."

"Come along, mama. And please, behave yourself at the dinner table."

"Am I to be scolded like a child? When did the roles reverse?"

"When you started ganging up on my guests," Bicky said.

"And what of my pound of flesh?" the Dowager demanded.

Slowing her pace, Evie asked Tom, "Do we have any idea why the police require our presence?"

Tom said, "Not so much mine, but, rather, yours. Because you might be able to identify the suspect."

"Me?" she mouthed. Evie pulled him back. "Since our arrival, we've been everywhere together. Why me specifically?"

Tom drew in a long breath.

"Are you trying to decide how much you can reveal to me?"

"Fine." He gave a nod of resignation. "Remember that fellow I told you I'd met at the pub?"

"Sir Bradford. Your generous benefactor who supplied you with clothes and a car." Had Tom found another Sir Bradford in London?

Tom nodded. "I asked him to keep an eye out. He called me while you were upstairs to say he'd noticed one of the locals driving around in a new car."

"A lot of people are getting cars these days. There's nothing unusual about that," Evie said.

"Not unless you don't have the means to acquire a new motor car. This fellow is a farmhand working for a local landowner."

"Perhaps someone left him some money." Evie rolled her eyes. "Fine, I'll go along with the theory I'm guessing you want to propose. Perhaps someone paid him for a job."

"Precisely. Anyhow, the police have questioned him and they believe they have their man."

"So where am I supposed to have seen this fellow?" Evie closed her eyes for a moment. "Oh… The day we arrived and I asked you to stop at the village. As I strode back to the car, I noticed someone watching me. A moment later, he took off at a run." And Tom had suggested someone might have been keeping an eye out for her. "I wonder if that's the man the police are referring to?"

Bicky returned to the drawing room and strode up to them. "I've been sent to herd you into the dining room. Are you two going to join us for dinner?"

"Yes, in a minute," Evie said and gave him a brief rundown of everything they'd been talking about.

Bicky crossed his arms. "I see. So, we might have the shooter behind bars. Does that mean the police are confident they'll find out who hired him?"

"That's my guess," Tom said.

"Why don't I feel relieved?" Evie asked. Since no one provided her with a possible reason, she went ahead and said, "Someone went to a lot of trouble. What if it's one of us?" She looked at Bicky. "What if it's…"

"Alexander. My heir," he said.

"I'm sorry, Bicky." Although, from the start he'd asked who stood to inherit…

Lady Gloriana came back into the drawing room. "What's going on?"

Before anyone could answer, Elizabeth walked back into the drawing room. "Have you all lost your appetites?"

"Bicky. I think you need to call the police," Evie suggested. With Clara so determined to get a divorce, Alexander must have realized Bicky would try to find another wife as soon as possible. He must have decided he couldn't take that risk. As long as Bicky remained married to Clara who had clearly failed to do her duty and provide him with an heir, Alexander would have been the next in line to inherit.

"Has dinner been cancelled?" Mark Harper asked from the doorway. "The Dowager is fretting."

Within the next few minutes, everyone had returned to the drawing room.

"I demand an explanation," the Dowager said. "In my time, these affairs were run with the utmost precision. Now everyone is scampering about willy-nilly."

"Bicky," Evie urged. "You must call the police. They have the possible shooter but you have your suspicions about Alexander. The sooner the police step in, the better. For all we know, he might be planning to strike again. If he's responsible for hiring the shooter, he'll be more dangerous than a wounded animal. He's bound to hear about the arrest and do something callous."

Stepping back, Evie looked in the general direction of the upstairs rooms. How bad could Penelope's headache be? Caro had been in her bedchamber and she hadn't even stirred. Swinging around again, she looked toward the other end of the house where she knew the kitchen was located. Penelope's maid sat in the kitchen. Caro had said she'd never seen her so upset.

"What is wrong with Evangeline Parker?" the Dowager asked. "She reminds of my cat, staring into space. Bicky, have you put something in the drinks? Everyone is behaving very strangely today. Starting with Lady Charlotte and her unfounded accusations. If news about it reached my ears, mark my word, it will have spread throughout the county."

A commotion outside the drawing room had everyone turning. The butler, Larkin, stumbled in. Or rather, he appeared to have been pushed in by Caro.

"Go ahead and announce me," Caro demanded in a hard whisper.

"Caro?" Evie stepped forward. "What's going on?"

"Milady. I'm sorry for bursting in like this…"

Evie waved her in. "What's happened?" Her maid appeared to be in a state of panic.

"It's Miss Shard. She's wailing. I can't make any sense out of what she's saying."

"Who is Miss Shard?" the Dowager asked.

"She's Lady Penelope's maid." Evie turned to Bicky and, for the third time, said, "You must call the police." She then hurried off with Caro who guided her down to the kitchen, Tom only a step behind them.

They found Miss Shard curled up in a corner, her hands covering her face as she mumbled and sobbed, "She told me to do it. She made me do it."

"Who made you do what?" Evie demanded.

Miss Shard wouldn't stop sobbing.

"I think we have to assume Penelope is the person who made her do something bad enough to reduce her to this." Evie grabbed hold of Tom's arm and led him out of the kitchen and up the stairs. As she hurried up the stairs, she said, "That journey to London must have something to do with this. I think Penelope might have done something she will live to regret."

Along the way, they nearly collided with a footman. When they reached Penelope's room, Evie didn't bother knocking. She barged in calling out Penelope's name. "Wake up." She reached the bed and grabbed Penelope by the shoulders only to gasp. Looking over her shoulder, she said, "There's something wrong. She's not responding." Her face looked pale and she'd obviously been sick.

Tom leaned in. After a moment, he stepped back. "She's gone."

Dr. Higgins wiped his hands. "You say she'd been complaining of a headache."

Evie nodded. "Since she arrived. Also, His Grace said she'd sounded confused. What happened to her?"

"I won't know for sure until we run some tests but I suspect she's been poisoned."

By now, everyone knew Lady Penelope had taken her last breath. With two attempts and now a death, Evie expected them to be in a quiet state of panic.

They followed Dr. Higgins down to the drawing

room. Everyone had settled down with cups of tea and sandwiches. The conversation, what little there was of it, remained muted.

Bicky strode up to them. "The Sergeant is still trying to get some sense out of Miss Shard."

Distracted, Evie said, "I suggest he search her pockets. If he doesn't find anything there, then he'll have to carry out a thorough search of the kitchen." Her gaze traveled from one guest to the other.

"What are you thinking?" Tom asked.

"Penelope didn't poison herself. According to Caro, she'd terrorized her maid. I think she might have pushed her too far." Turning to the doctor, she asked, "What sort of poison do you suspect?"

"I really cannot know for sure, but the symptoms you mentioned suggest she might have been poisoned with arsenic."

Larkin cleared his throat. "Your Grace, what would you like me to do about dinner?"

Bicky looked around the room. "I think we have all lost our appetites, Larkin."

Dr. Higgins excused himself saying, "The ambulance should be arriving soon to… take her away."

Evie took a moment to settle her thumping heart. Belatedly, she remembered thinking she should call in on Penelope to check on her. Would it have made a difference?

"Miss Shard spent the afternoon in the kitchen,"

Evie murmured. She grabbed hold of Tom's sleeve. "Miss Shard. Remember what she said?"

"She made me do it." Tom must have read the panic in her eyes. Looking at Bicky, he said, "It might be a good idea if you dispose of the food. If Miss Shard poisoned Penelope, she might have tampered with the rest of the food too."

Everyone within hearing gasped and that set off a murmured conversation as they all asked for explanations.

The Dowager sprung to her feet. "The food... poisoned?" She promptly took her cup of tea to a table and set it down. "I'm suddenly feeling faint." A footman helped her to a chair.

Still holding on to Tom's sleeve, Evie drew him aside. "She made me do it. How can we possibly interpret that? I doubt it means Penelope issued an order for Miss Shard to poison her. Could it mean Penelope pushed her too far? According to Caro, Miss Shard suffered terribly and had been constantly reprimanded by Penelope."

"Everyone has a breaking point," Tom mused.

"What if someone else put her up to it?"

"Do you have someone in mind?"

"Not really, but... we know Penelope went to see Alexander. What if she could provide proof of his involvement in the attempt on Bicky's life?" Alexander would want to get rid of anyone who could point the finger at him.

Tom shook his head. "I didn't know Lady Penelope, but something tells me she would have shared the information. What reason could she possibly have to harm Bicky?"

None, Evie thought. Then again...

"She might have been beyond reason. Lord Hammond must have made his intentions clear to her. Who knows what went through her mind." Crossing her arms, Evie strode to the window. "Either Miss Shard worked alone or she took orders from someone. I'm convinced Alexander Fleshling is responsible for plotting against Bicky. He is the one with the most to gain and lose."

Someone behind them cleared his throat. Turning, they saw Sergeant Newbury standing by the door to the drawing room. Tom approached him.

"I wonder if I might have a word with His Grace."

When Bicky joined them, the Sergeant said, "I have alerted Scotland Yard. Miss Shard has confessed." The Sergeant looked around the room. "I would strongly suggest avoiding the consumption of any food. It seems you had all been targeted..."

A collective gasp made its way around the drawing room.

CHAPTER 26

A cup of poison?

"Poor Bicky. I suppose he will now have to agree to a divorce and find himself a proper wife."

Evie felt too dazed to bother looking up to see who had spoken.

"To think, if he'd had an heir none of this would have happened…" someone else remarked.

"Were the sandwiches safe to eat?"

"And the tea…"

Evie settled down with a cup of tea. Scotland Yard Detectives had taken Alexander Fleshling into custody. The police had Miss Shard's confession but Evie wondered if that would be enough to put Alexander behind bars.

According to Miss Shard, Alexander had approached her the previous Christmas when he'd stayed at Yarborough Manor. The plan had been to poison the food.

Elizabeth's face looked pale and her voice sounded strained when she said, "To think, we should all be dead now."

Evie shook her head. "I cannot believe the lengths he'd been prepared to go to in order to cover his tracks."

"What do you mean?" Bicky asked.

"Why else poison food we were all going to eat unless he wanted to cover his tracks?" It made sense to Evie. Killing everyone reduced the risk of suspicion falling on Alexander. If Bicky had been the only victim, as the heir, the police would have questioned Alexander Fleshling. However, with everyone dead, only one person would have been held accountable. The most susceptible one. Miss Shard. "Who knows what Alexander had planned for her."

"But Miss Shard insists she didn't poison Penelope," Bicky said.

Evie got up and strode around the drawing room. "Penelope went to see Alexander. Perhaps he delivered the poison." Turning, she looked at Dr. Higgins who'd been called back to attend to the Dowager who had felt faint. Evie told him what time Penelope had caught the train and Bicky confirmed her time of arrival at Yarborough Manor. "She complained of a headache. Would the time it took to travel from London be enough for the poison to take effect?"

Dr. Higgins nodded. "Yes, but it all really depends on the dosage."

The Dowager pressed her hand to her throat. "Miss Shard has been in this house for days. She might have been slowly poisoning us." She looked at Bicky. "Either you produce an heir yourself or you let anyone who thinks they stand a chance fight it out among themselves. Monarchs have died without naming an heir. Why not you?"

The next morning, Evie and Tom were the only ones to join Bicky for breakfast.

"We'll be setting out for the police station this morning," Evie said as she helped herself to some bacon and eggs.

"Are you sure you're up to it?" Tom asked.

"Absolutely. Although, I doubt it will make any difference. Alexander must have taken precautions. He's not likely to have dealt with the shooter himself."

"And yet he enlisted Miss Shard's help," Tom reasoned.

"I wonder if he had plans for her." Evie took a sip of her coffee. "I trust the police will be able to prove he poisoned Penelope. Surely, there is no such thing as a perfect crime. Someone procured the poison. Speaking of which..." She looked at Tom's plate. "Have you lost your appetite?"

"I had some toast. The butler assured us the bread had been freshly baked early this morning."

Evie laughed. "I'm sure the eggs were cracked today."

Tom looked toward the platter. "You have a point." Getting up, he helped himself to some scrambled eggs.

"I suppose the others have decided to fast." She set her fork down. "Oh, heavens. Has anyone checked on them?"

Bicky nodded. "At the crack of dawn. Everyone made it through the night."

She couldn't help noticing Bicky's tone lacked his usual convivial chirpiness. Then again, one of his close friends had been killed and his heir had tried to kill him and all his friends.

"I suppose you should know," Bicky said, "I have decided to go ahead and begin divorce proceedings. I can't help but feel partly responsible for poor Penelope's death."

"Nonsense," Evie said.

"If I hadn't been so stubborn, then Clara would not have dragged Lord Hammond into this mess."

"If not Clara then someone else would have done the deed," Evie said. "I wouldn't be surprised to discover Lord Hammond has been straying for quite some time. But then, that's guesswork on my part."

"There's nothing wrong with your guesswork," Tom remarked.

Bicky picked up his newspaper. "At least there's no mention of this nasty business in today's newspaper. But I suppose I'll have to brace myself."

Smiling, Evie said, "We shall have to see if we can pick up some newspapers from home. I'm ever so eager to read the sports pages."

"I didn't realize you were interested in sport," Bicky said.

"Oh, not usually but as I recently informed Tom, I am partial to the Yankees." Smiling at Tom, she said, "I'm ready when you are. On our way back, we'll have to stop at *Marceline's Salon de Beaute*. I'd like to pick up some more of their lovely soap before we leave."

"Are you sure you want to do this? Going to the police station is not for the fainthearted... I don't mean to imply you're faint of heart, but you don't have to."

"Oh, but I must. It's a matter of duty."

EPILOGUE

The road home...

"I look forward to your next visit and promise to do my best to make it as boring as possible."

"Oh, I doubt you could ever manage that, Bicky." With the shooter identified as the man Evie had seen in the village, the police had managed to connect him to Alexander Fleshling. Bicky had lost his heir. Alexander had been taken into custody to await trial. According to Sergeant Newbury, they already had enough evidence to prove his involvement in Lady Penelope's death. It seemed Alexander's chauffeur had been well-informed and quite willing to save his own neck.

Looking up at the splendid manor house, Evie said, "I expect to receive an invitation to your next wedding." While divorce proceedings would take some time, she suspected Clara would use all her connections to expedite matters.

Evie said her goodbyes and strode toward the motor car. As she waited for Caro to make her final inspection of the luggage, she said, "Tom, remember what you said at the start about sticking as close as possible to the truth?"

Tom looked away.

"Don't pretend you didn't hear me."

Releasing a long breath, he looked at her. "Yes, I remember."

"Well, exactly how much of what you said can we rely on to be true?"

He dropped his gaze and subjected his shoes to a close scrutiny.

"Were you a wildcatter?"

"I think there's a wildcatter in all of us."

"Now you're being deliberately elusive," she chided. "Do I need to place an advertisement for a new chauffeur?"

"I hope you won't. The job suits me, at least for the time being."

"I see. Are you entertaining other ideas?"

He held her gaze for a long moment. "I think I'm beginning to learn to go with the flow."

"I'm glad to hear that because you might have to dispense with your chauffeur's uniform."

He gave her a small smile. "At least until we're out of sight of Yarborough Manor." He held the car door open for her. "For now, everyone thinks your chauffeur has been taken ill and I've offered to drive you home."

"You have an answer for everything. I'm so glad you're on my team. Then again, you're not really... How do you think the Red Sox will manage without Babe Ruth?"

"I suppose we'll just have to wait and see."

With a final wave goodbye, they drove off. Evie fixed her attention on the road ahead only to slide it over to Tom.

"Caro, please remind me to write a note to my granny. I need to thank her..."

I hope you have enjoyed reading House Party Murder Rap. Next in the series: Murder at the Tea Party.

If you wish to receive news about my new releases:

Follow Sonia Parin on Bookbub

AUTHOR NOTES

FACTS AND HISTORICAL REFERENCES

As I set out to write my first historical mystery, I realized I would have to pay close attention to my word choices. In my effort to ensure the story remained historically correct, I spent many hours checking and double-checking word and phrase usage. Here are some examples:

Week-end, 1630s, from week + end. Originally a northern word (referring to the period from Saturday noon to Monday morning); it became general after 1878.

Getaway, 1852, "an escape," originally in fox hunting, from verbal phrase get away "escape". Of prisoners or criminals from 1893.

Pot-hole, 1826, originally a geological feature in glaciers and gravel beds. Applied to a hole in a road from 1909.

Like a bat out of hell: The Lions of the Lord: A Tale of the Old West By Harry Leon Wilson, Copyright 1903, published June, 1903, page 107 (google book full view):

Why, I tell you, young man, if I knew any places where the pinches was at, you'd see me comin' the other way like a bat out of hell.

Also...

Tom Winchester's background: In Chapter Eight, Tom Winchester claims: "Back in 1914, I started out as a wildcatter in Tulsa, Oklahoma. Soon after, I purchased my first drilling rights."

I borrowed this information from John Paul Getty's own start in the oil business.

Baseball

May 1, 1920: Babe Ruth's first Yankee home run is a 'colossal clout' against Red Sox. As the second month of the 1920 season opened, the New York Yankees routed the Boston Red Sox at the Polo Grounds, 6-0, behind Babe Ruth's first home run as a New Yorker.

Printed in Great Britain
by Amazon